This

GENIE IN A TRAP

To

Ciaran Murtagh is a writer and actor. His first book, *Dinopants*, was published by Piccadilly Press and was followed by three sequels. He also writes TV shows and has recently been involved with scripting *The Slammer*, *The 4 O'Clock Club*, *Diddy Movies*, *The Legend of Dick and Dom*, *Scoop*, *Hotel Trubble*, and *Dennis and Gnasher*. He regularly appears in TV shows for CBBC and can be seen in every series of *The Slammer* and in *Dick and Dom's Hoopla*.

He lives in London with his wife and secret sweetie cupboard and has a lovely daughter called Eleanor. He is an unapologetic fan of the music of a-ha and still sucks his thumb. It is unclear which of these two facts is more embarrassing to his friends and family.

Find out more at www.ciaranmurtagh.com

Also in the *Genie* series:
Genie in Training
Genie in Trouble

Other books by Ciaran Murtagh:

Dinopants
Dinopoo
Dinoburps
Dinoball

CIARAN MURTAGH

GENIE IN A TRAP

Illustrated by
Adria Meserve

Piccadilly Press • London

For Theo and Jake
Thanks for being the first
to read everything I write!

First published in Great Britain in 2013
by Piccadilly Press Ltd,
5 Castle Road, London NW1 8PR
www.piccadillypress.co.uk

Text copyright © Ciaran Murtagh, 2013
Illustrations copyright © Adria Meserve, 2013

A catalogue record for this book is available
from the British Library

ISBN: 978 1 84812 312 0 (paperback)

1 3 5 7 9 10 8 6 4 2

Printed in the UK by CPI Group (UK), Croydon, CR0 4TD
Cover design by Simon Davis
Cover and interior illustrations by Adria Meserve

CHAPTER 1

Jamie Quinn gasped in surprise when a pair of hands pushed him from the plane. His eyes grew wide with terror as he plummeted towards the ground. The squeal of the plane's engines faded away and the sound of rushing wind filled his ears. He clenched his teeth, closed his eyes and fell headfirst through the clouds.

The headphones in Jamie's crash helmet gave a

burst of static and sparked into life. 'Isn't this brilliant?' came the crackling voice of his best friend, Dylan Reid. 'No!' said Jamie through his own helmet microphone. 'I shouldn't even be here. It was *your* wish to go skydiving.' 'We're best friends,' said Dylan, with a laugh. 'We do everything together!'

'Lucky me!' mumbled Jamie sarcastically.

Dylan had been given three wishes when he had released Jamie's genie friend, Balthazar Najar, from a bottle at the bottom of the sea. He'd always wanted to skydive and so it was his first wish – and he'd wanted Jamie to share the experience, so that was why they were currently hundreds of metres up in the air, hurtling towards the ground.

Dylan gave Jamie a cheeky
wave and stuck out his arms.
'Wheeeeee!' He laughed as he
swooped across the sky. 'Is it a bird? Is it a plane?
No, it's SuperDylan!'

Jamie's house
looked like a model and the
cars in his street looked like toys, but the ground
was getting closer by the second.

'Pull your ripcord,' Dylan instructed Jamie
through the headphones. 'We don't want to be
turned into pavement pizzas!'

Jamie and Dylan pulled the straps and their parachutes unfurled above them. Yanking on two red steering handles, Jamie did his best to guide himself into his back garden. He glided over the fence towards a patch of soft grass, but a sudden gust of wind blew him towards the trampoline instead. He landed on it with a *boing* and bounced straight back into the air.

'Argh!' Jamie screamed, and landed in the leafy branches of a nearby oak.

'*Tree*-mendous landing, Jamie!' said Dylan. He was laughing so hard he forgot to steer and crashed into the fishpond.

'At least I won't need a bath tonight,' he spluttered, spitting water onto the grass like a novelty gnome.

Just then Balthazar appeared in a puff of smoke. He was wearing his usual tattered red pantaloons and a matching waistcoat. 'How was that?' he asked. 'Ripcord or rip-bored? Rip-*bored* — geddit?!' Balthazar laughed at his own terrible joke, and laughed even harder when he saw Jamie dangling upside-down from the tree. 'You look like an abandoned Action Man!'

'Get me down,' shouted Jamie, kicking his legs.

'Keep your hair on!' said Balthazar. 'You'll panic the pigeons!'

The genie inhaled deeply, his chest expanding like a balloon, as he chanted a magical rhyme.
'Leaves of green and bark of brown,
Help me get poor Jamie down.'

When it looked as if he was ready to pop, Balthazar blew out a breath that shone with sparkles, and the shimmering cloud surrounded Jamie's body.

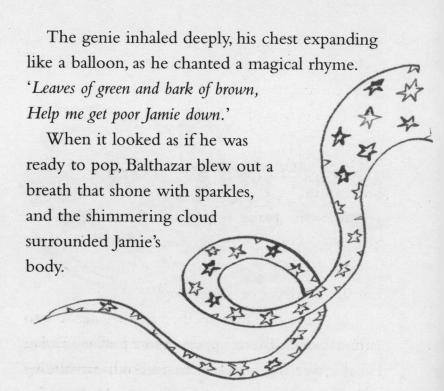

Suddenly a branch magically came to life and flicked Jamie onto the ground like a boy-sized bogey.

'Oof!' said Jamie, landing in a heap.

'Sorry,' said Balthazar. 'That wasn't exactly what I had in mind.'

Jamie dusted himself down as he got to his feet, and smiled. He was used to Balthazar's wishes not always going according to plan.

Behind them, Dylan clambered out of the fishpond and sneezed.

'Let's get you dry before you catch cold,' said Jamie.

'Allow me,' said Balthazar, preparing to wish once again.

'No!' said Jamie quickly. 'I think we've had enough of your wishes for the time being.'

'Yeah,' said Dylan. 'You might turn me into a human hairdryer or something!'

The three of them laughed as they went into Jamie's house. Jamie sat on his bed while Dylan dried himself with a towel and Balthazar fiddled with Jamie's racing car moneybox. Suddenly coins spilt onto the floor.

'Oops,' said Balthazar, handing the moneybox back to Jamie. 'I think it needs a pit stop!'

Jamie rolled his eyes as Balthazar blew a sparkling wish to put the coins back. Coins flew through the air, and Jamie had to dive out of the way as a flying five pence piece zipped past his ear and into the money slot.

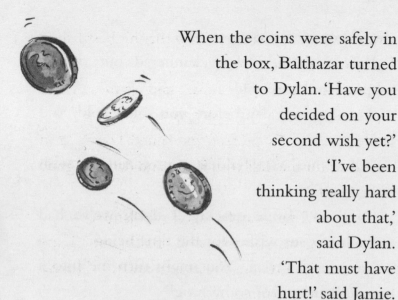

When the coins were safely in the box, Balthazar turned to Dylan. 'Have you decided on your second wish yet?' 'I've been thinking really hard about that,' said Dylan. 'That must have hurt!' said Jamie.

Dylan gave him a playful dig in the ribs. 'And I've decided that I want to go to the Genie Academy, just like Jamie.'

Jamie had once spent a whole term at the Genie Academy in the genie land of Lampville-upon-Cloud. He'd found out all about the genie way of life and he'd even learnt a bit of magic. As he was still a trainee genie, his magic only worked in Lampville – to avoid accidents you weren't allowed to practise wishing in the human world until you were fully qualified. He'd been telling Dylan about his adventures ever since he'd returned, so it wasn't surprising that his best friend wanted to see for himself.

'But you can't go now,' said Jamie. 'We're supposed to be having a sleepover!'

'That's why it's perfect,' explained Dylan. 'You can cover for me. Tell your mum and dad I've gone to bed early.'

'But you'll be away for ages,' said Jamie.

'No he won't,' corrected Balthazar. 'Time moves much faster up there, remember? I'll have him back by morning.'

It was true. Jamie had spent weeks in the Academy but had only been gone one night on Earth.

'Although my parents would be more likely to believe you're off visiting a magical land high in the clouds than the idea that you've gone to bed early!' said Jamie.

Dylan laughed and gave his friend a hug. 'Thanks, mate,' he said. 'I owe you one!'

'What are we waiting for?' said Balthazar, clapping his hands in delight.

'I wish to go to the Genie Academy,' said Dylan,

barely able to keep the excitement from his voice.

Balthazar inhaled deeply and blew a cloud of sparkling stars towards Dylan. When the cloud evaporated, Dylan and Balthazar were gone.

Jamie leant back on his bed and tried to read a book, but his mind kept thinking about the adventures he was sure Dylan and Balthazar were having without him. He wondered whether Dylan would get to ride on a magic carpet or manage to wish up a bowl of cloud ice cream. In the genie world, everything was made from clouds, even food. Jamie laughed as he remembered the first time he'd tried to wish up a sandwich and the bread had zoomed around the dinner hall like a rocket! Thankfully Methuzular, the kindly headmaster of the Academy, had wished it back to his plate.

Jamie shut his book. It was no use trying to read. The memories of his wonderful adventures were better than any story! The last time Jamie had met Methuzular, he'd rescued him from Lampville Jail and together with Jamie's gran, who turned out to be Methuzular's long lost sister, they had defeated the two evil genies who had put him there – Dakhil

Ganim and his son Dabir. The nasty pair were banished to a bottle at the bottom of the sea for their crimes, and no one ever expected them to be released from there.

Jamie's memories were punctured by a loud 'Hi-yah!' from outside. Jamie poked his head out of the window to see Josh, the youngest of the three brothers who lived next door, pick up his middle brother Will and throw him onto the grass.

'Doesn't that hurt?' called Jamie.

'No,' said Will, picking himself off the ground. 'It's judo. We'll teach you if you like!'

Jamie reckoned he could do with the distraction – he felt a bit jealous of Dylan in Lampville-upon-Cloud. He grinned and ran down the stairs.

As he arrived in the garden, the sound of crashing cymbals filled the air. Oliver, the eldest brother, had started his drumming practice.

Before Jamie could catch his breath, Josh had grabbed his T-shirt. 'Hold on tight,' he said.

Josh swept his leg to one side and Jamie felt himself tumbling through the air. Even though Josh was only seven years old, he flipped Jamie like a pro. Jamie picked himself up, and the brothers showed him some of their judo moves. Soon they were all yelling and flipping each other all over the garden. Baxter, the boys' excitable border terrier, barked in delight.

Oliver stopped his drumming and peered out of the window. 'Keep it down out there,' he snapped. 'I'm trying to practise!'

'The cheek of it!' huffed Will, as Oliver returned to bashing his drumkit. '*Him* telling *us* to keep it down!'

At the far end of the garden, Baxter was barking at the hedge.

'What is that dog up to now?' asked Josh.

Baxter's tail was wagging like a furry windscreen wiper, so Jamie went to investigate. When he peered through the branches he had to suppress a shout – Balthazar and Dylan were peering back at him!

Balthazar grabbed Jamie and pulled him into the hedge. 'You need to come back to Lampville,' he hissed. 'Now!'

CHAPTER 2

Balthazar and Dylan took an arm each and dragged Jamie further into the hedge.

'Hey!' said Jamie with a laugh. 'What's the emergency? Is Methuzular's beard on fire or something?'

Balthazar and Dylan exchanged a strange look.

'No,' said Balthazar, shaking his head.

'It was supposed to be funny,' explained Jamie patiently, giving his friends a curious stare. It was unlike Balthazar not to giggle at a joke, even one as bad as that!

Suddenly Balthazar began to laugh – the sort of laugh you make when you don't quite get a joke. Balthazar gave Dylan a dig in the ribs and he joined in. His laugh sounded strange too – nothing like the playful chuckle Jamie was used to hearing.

Something weird was going on. Why were they acting so strangely? Jamie was about to open his mouth to ask when he heard a rustle in the bushes behind him.

'Are you all right in there, Jamie?'

It was Josh coming to see where he had gone.

Jamie thought fast. 'I'm fine,' he called. 'Baxter just found an old tennis ball.'

'Rubbish! You're trying to escape the judo master!' said Josh.

Jamie's heart began to thump. He couldn't let Josh spot Balthazar and Dylan or he'd start asking awkward questions. What was he going to do?

Just then the kitchen door opened and Josh's mum shouted into the garden.

'Josh! Will! Time for tea!'

'Sorry, Jamie!' said Josh. 'Gotta go! It's pizza tonight!'

Jamie breathed a sigh of relief as the two brothers raced up the garden path. When he heard the kitchen door close, he turned back to his friends. Normally he would have loved an excuse to return to the Academy, but something fishy was going on, he was sure of it. Jamie needed answers.

'You drag me into a hedge,' said Jamie, 'laugh like weirdos and want me to come back to Lampville . . . There's something you're not telling me. What's wrong?'

Balthazar and Dylan exchanged a furtive glance.

'Nothing's wrong at all. It's good news, but . . . we're not supposed to tell you,' said Balthazar quietly.

'It's a secret,' agreed Dylan.

Their voices sounded dreamy and faraway. Neither of them were very good at keeping secrets usually, thought Jamie. Maybe that was why they were acting so strangely.

'What secret?' he asked.

'You promise you won't tell?' asked Balthazar.

Jamie crossed his heart.

'You're going to be guest of honour at the Academy end of year party,' whispered Balthazar. 'And best of all, Methuzular wants to unveil a statue of you in the Great Hall.'

'It's as a thank you for all the good work you've

done for genies,' added
Dylan.

Suddenly all thoughts of
Balthazar and Dylan's
strange behaviour
disappeared as Jamie's heart
swelled with pride. To have
a statue in the Great Hall

was one of the
greatest honours a
genie could receive. He
couldn't believe he'd
been chosen!
'M-m-me?' he
stammered.
'Are you sure?'
Balthazar and
Dylan nodded.
'You saved
Methuzular's life,'
continued Balthazar.

'And got Dakhil and Dabir banished. You deserve it!'

It was true – on his last visit to the Academy, Jamie had found the place in turmoil. Dakhil Ganim was headmaster at the Academy and, together with his son Dabir, had planned to turn humans into genie slaves. It had been up to Jamie to expose Dakhil's plot and get things back to normal. But he hadn't saved the genies all on his own – he'd had a lot of help from his genie friends and his gran. Surely they should get statues too?

Then a different thought struck Jamie – he couldn't go back even if he wanted to. He and Dylan were supposed to be having a sleepover. He needed to be there to tell his parents Dylan had gone to bed early. His parents were going to be suspicious enough about that. They couldn't both disappear.

'I can't come,' said Jamie sadly. 'I'm covering for Dylan, remember?'

A dark cloud seemed to flicker across Balthazar's face and he grabbed Jamie's arm. 'You have to!' he said. 'We can't go back without you! Everyone will be disappointed.'

'Balthazar!' gasped Jamie in surprise. 'What's got into you? There's no need to pull my arm off!'

Balthazar released Jamie's arm and Jamie gave it a rub. There were five red marks where Balthazar had gripped him.

'Ask your gran,' Dylan said. 'She'll cover for both of us. She knows all about the genie world – she used to be one after all.'

Jamie looked at his two friends and nodded. They were right. He couldn't miss the unveiling of his statue; it would be an insult to the genies. 'OK, wait here.'

He crawled out of the hedge and scurried back home to find Gran hanging out the washing in the garden.

'Gran!' he called as he ran towards her.

Gran dropped the pair of boxer shorts she was pegging to the line. They were black and covered in bright red hearts.

'You nearly gave me a heart attack!' she said, bending down to pick them up. 'And they're your dad's lucky pair too!' Gran tossed the pants back into the washing basket and turned to Jamie. 'What's got into you?' she asked.

'I have to go back to the Academy,' explained Jamie. 'Apparently Methuzular is planning to unveil a statue of me in the Great Hall!'

Gran took a step back in surprise and toppled into the washing basket. 'A statue of you in the

Great Hall?' she gasped. 'What an honour!'

'I need to go now. Dylan's coming too, so can you make up an excuse to Mum and Dad for us not being around?'

Gran thought for a moment and then nodded her head. 'But be careful, Jamie,' she warned. 'Make sure you're back by morning.'

'No worries,' said Jamie, giving Gran a thank-you kiss on the cheek as he helped her up.

'Give my love to Methuzular!' she called, waving him off with one of Jamie's dad's polka-dot hankies.

Jamie ran back to the hedge where Balthazar and Dylan were

standing just as he'd left them. 'She'll cover for us,' he said, smiling.

'Get changed, then.' Balthazar handed Jamie a red genie outfit, which he quickly put on. 'The Portal of Dreams is right here,' said Balthazar, moving a bushy branch back to reveal a shimmering image of an Academy classroom.

The Portal of Dreams was a magical gateway that connected the human and genie worlds. The genies used it like an interactive television set to keep an eye on humans, but if they needed to get to Earth quickly, they could simply step through its surface.

'Everyone's waiting for you,' said Dylan. 'Look!'

Through the rippling portal, Jamie could see his genie friend Adeel Maloof and the smiling face of Methuzular. They were both waving to him, and Jamie couldn't help but grin. It would be good to see them again and go back to the Academy.

He stepped through the portal. For a moment he had one foot in the garden and another in the Academy, and he paused, thinking how odd it was to be half in one world and half in another.

A rough shove broke his thoughts, and Jamie tumbled through the portal onto the ground. He picked himself up and turned to protest at having been pushed so hard, but neither Dylan nor Balthazar were anywhere to be seen.

Jamie looked around. He was standing in one of the Academy classrooms. Methuzular and Adeel were still waving, and he ran towards them. But as Jamie threw his arms around the friendly pair to give them a hug, his hands passed straight through them and they disappeared in a puff of smoke.

Suddenly the lights blacked out and Jamie jumped as a door clanged shut. Firey torches burst into flame and Jamie looked around in the dim light. The classroom had disappeared! Instead, he was standing in a small, square cage in the middle of a vast cavern.

'Help!' he screamed, grabbing the cage bars. 'Balthazar! Dylan! Help!'

A booming cackle filled the cave. It bounced

off the walls like the laughter of a ghost train vampire.

'I hope you enjoyed our little trick, Jamie Najar,' chuckled the voice. 'I'm afraid there is no party . . . no statue . . . and no escape.'

'Balthazar!' Jamie shouted in panic, looking around frantically for his friends. 'Dylan!'

A cloaked figure emerged from the shadows

and strode towards the cage. 'You don't get it, do you? They're on my side now!'

Jamie watched in disbelief as Balthazar and Dylan stepped out of the gloom and stood behind the mysterious figure like obedient servants. The figure stopped at the edge of the cage, and as the light from the flickering torches caught his face, Jamie shuddered in terror. He was staring into the cold black eyes of Dakhil Ganim!

CHAPTER 3

Jamie backed away as Dakhil gripped the cage bars and peered at him with all the glee of a snake about to devour a mouse.

'We meet again,' he said, licking his lips. 'There's someone else who will be pleased to see you, too!'

Dakhil clapped twice and a young genie hurried to his side.

'You remember Dabir, don't you?' said Dakhil with a cruel smirk. 'He's missed you!'

Jamie shuddered. Dabir was just as unpleasant as his father and had tried to make Jamie's life at the Academy a misery with mean wishes.

Dabir thrust a hand through the bars and gripped Jamie's waistcoat, pulling him close. Jamie felt the cold bars pressing into his cheek. 'We've got plans for you, Jamie Najar,' hissed Dabir menacingly.

'B–b–but you were banished,' stammered Jamie. 'To a bottle at the bottom of the sea. How did you escape?'

Dakhil placed a hand on his son's shoulder and Dabir released Jamie.

'We have your two friends to thank for that,' said Dakhil, pointing a bony finger at Balthazar and Dylan.

Jamie shook his head. 'They'd never release you!' he said. 'They'd die first!'

'Apparently not. To think all these years I wanted to get rid of Balthazar Najar,' he said. 'Yet without his bumbling ways, I wouldn't be here now. He released us, Jamie, you can be sure of that. When we found ourselves free from the bottle Dabir and I were as amazed as you! So we made Balthazar tell us exactly how it happened – and a very interesting and entertaining story it was too! Dylan was apparently full of questions about Dabir and myself when he arrived at the Academy.'

'Apparently you'd talked about us so much, he wanted to know more, and hear about all our crimes and the wishes we'd twisted,' sneered Dabir.

'Balthazar just couldn't resist taking Dylan to see us trapped in the bottle,' continued Dakhil. 'He was so proud that you managed to expose our plans and get us punished. Being the Academy caretaker, he has a key that opens every door in the

Academy so he can clean the rooms after lessons. He used the key to get into Methuzular's office and find the secret file that recorded the exact location of our bottle. So one morning, just before school, Balthazar took Dylan through the portal to a desolate island in the middle of a deep ocean. Dylan waited on the island while Balthazar fetched us from the depths.'

'Balthazar didn't think there'd be any harm in it,' sniggered Dabir. 'After all, we were safely trapped inside the bottle, weren't we? Balthazar also wanted to show off to his new human friend. Little did he know it was all about to go horribly wrong!'

'When we saw him swimming towards us, we couldn't believe our eyes,' said Dakhil. 'When he carried us to shore we thought he'd gone mad. Turns out he was just stupid. The pair of them peered in at us as Balthazar explained all about the terrible things we'd done over the years.'

'Dylan seemed fit to burst with rage,' said Dabir, his eyes sparkling with delight. 'Especially when he heard how I had trapped you in a lamp and wanted to keep you as a pet. He spluttered and fumed and stamped his feet and eventually he shouted, "I wish those two were standing right in front of me so I could give them a piece of my mind!"'

Jamie shook his head and slumped to the ground. Dylan had always had a fearsome temper and he could guess what was coming next.

'Before Dylan had even realised what he had said, Balthazar was granting the wish,' explained Dakhil. 'Dylan tried to stop him but the bottle was already shrouded in sparkles.'

'Dylan had one wish left and Balthazar couldn't refuse to grant it!' giggled Dabir. 'Your idiot human friend accidentally wished us free and the other idiot made it happen!'

Dakhil and Dabir collapsed into laughter and Jamie pressed his hands to his forehead. Balthazar was always granting wishes without thinking. It was why he got into so much trouble. He once turned a maths teacher into a scary monster because he wished he had eyes in the back of his head. The children had been so scared they'd stayed away from school for a month! Another time Balthazar had turned a baby's mum into a mannequin because she was crying for a dummy. It had taken a lot of genie magic to put that one right.

But this time, Jamie realised, Balthazar had had no choice. He *had* to grant Dylan's wish once it had been made. It was the fifth rule of the Genie Code.

Rule one:
do not steal from another genie.

Rule two:
do not use your wishes for evil.

Rule three:
never back down from a genie challenge.

Rule four:

always obey your master when tied to
a lamp, teapot or bottle.

Rule five:

grant every wish your master asks.

Breaking one of the rules was a banishable offence. The first time you broke the rules you were banished to a lamp, the second time to a teapot and the third time to a bottle at the bottom of the sea where you were unlikely ever to get out.

Through silly mistakes, Balthazar had broken the code twice before so he was on his third and final warning. If he hadn't granted Dylan's wish, he could have been banished to a bottle himself.

Jamie peered through the bars at the pair of cackling genies and shook his head in despair. What had his friends done?

'We always knew we'd be released eventually,' said Dakhil.

'We had thought it would take a few hundred

years for us to get washed up on the shore,' said Dabir.

'But we vowed to be ready when it happened,' said Dakhil. 'Which is why we'd been practising a special wish we found in the Book of Wishes.'

The Book of Wishes was the most powerful book in the genie world. It contained the details of every wish ever granted. The book was kept by the headmaster of the Academy, but when Methuzular had been imprisoned, Dakhil had made himself headmaster and gained access to the book. Jamie had managed to get the Book of Wishes back from Dakhil, but it seemed Dakhil had taken the time to learn its most powerful secrets.

'We found a hypno-wish,' continued Dakhil. 'A wish so powerful it can make a genie or human do whatever you command! It's a tricky one to get right, but we had the time to practise in the bottle, and nothing else to do but plan our revenge. The moment we were free again, we cast the wish on Balthazar and Dylan, our words floating into their ears and affecting their minds, turning them into our slaves. Now they'll do whatever we say. Watch!'

Dakhil turned and spoke to Balthazar. 'Servant! Bring me my staff!'

Jamie could only look on as Balthazar fetched Dakhil's long wooden staff like an obedient puppy.

Dabir turned to Dylan. 'Dylan!' he ordered. 'Rub my feet.'

Dylan bent down, tugged off Dabir's shoes and began to massage Dabir's disgustingly flakey feet. Jamie was almost sick.

'When we told them to trick you into coming back, they had no choice but to obey,' gloated Dabir.

Jamie gripped the cage bars. 'I knew they were behaving strangely! But I'd have come back anyway, even if I had guessed it was a trap. I wouldn't have left them knowing they were in trouble.'

Dakhil raised an eyebrow and gave Jamie an appraising look. It was one part admiration but two parts hatred.

'Maybe you *are* as brave as people say, Jamie

Najar,' said Dakhil, 'but it won't do you any good. You are locked in a cage without any hope of escape. Balthazar and Dylan are just the start of our plan. Soon my hypno-wish will infect every single genie in Lampville! But the best thing about the hypno-wish is its power . . . Unlike most genie wishes, it doesn't wear off quickly, but can last for many years. The only way to remove it is by reversing it and that is very tricky indeed!'

A shiver ran down Jamie's spine as he imagined all the terrible things a pair of genies like Dakhil and Dabir could do with an army of servant genies on their side.

'Oh yes,' said Dakhil, nodding his head. 'Revenge is going to taste very sweet indeed. Soon even the great Methuzular will obey my every command and, best of all . . .' Dakhil's eyes glinted in the darkness. '. . . *you* are going to be the one to betray him!'

'Never!' snapped Jamie, banging the cell bars in anger.

'We'll soon see about that,' cackled Dakhil, turning on his heel as Dabir followed behind him.

Jamie looked at Balthazar and Dylan, but they just stood there like zombies. He couldn't believe the terror they had unleashed. Jamie slumped to the ground. The cloud cage towered high above him and the barred roof cast long shadows across the floor.

Jamie's heart sank. Dakhil was right – there was no escape.

CHAPTER 4

Jamie watched through the cage bars as Dakhil and Dabir busied themselves in the cavern. Every now and then the sound of clanking chains filled the air, but Jamie couldn't see much. What were they up to?

Suddenly Jamie had an idea. While at the Academy he had learnt all sorts of wishes. He had managed to make delicious ice cream out of clouds, learnt how to float in the air and had even saved a lady from certain death by shrinking her foot! A thought struck him. If he could make a foot shrink, why couldn't he make his whole body shrink too? Then he would be able to squeeze through the bars, escape and raise the alarm. Jamie's genie magic didn't work when he was away from the genie world, but now he was back there was nothing to stop him!

Jamie closed his eyes and tried to take his mind to that special place where magic could happen. He breathed in deeply, concentrated hard and prepared to shroud himself in a shimmering wish cloud.

Just as he was about to blow out, Dabir's voice shattered his concentration.

'Don't even bother!' said Dabir.

Jamie opened his eyes. The menacing genie was striding towards him.

'These bars are lined with thunderclouds. You know what that means, don't you?'

Jamie's heart sank. He knew exactly what that meant. Wishes did not work in thunderclouds.

'Did you really think we'd be that stupid?' sneered Dabir. 'Wishes won't help you here.'

Dabir returned to his work and Jamie punched the floor in frustration. He wasn't going to get out that way. If he wanted to escape then he'd need Balthazar and Dylan's help.

Jamie gripped the bars and hissed in their direction. 'Balthazar! Dylan!'

Dylan and Balthazar turned to look at Jamie, and for a moment he hoped they might be about to help him, but when he looked into their eyes he knew that was never going to happen. They looked blank, as if they had never seen Jamie before.

'Save your breath!' called Dakhil. 'They only obey two voices in the world and neither of them is yours! They will stand like that, patiently waiting for instructions, until Dabir or I command otherwise – we cast the hypno-wish on them, so they will only listen to us. When they go about their orders, a little of their personality returns, but only enough to complete the task in hand.'

Jamie fixed Dakhil with a fierce stare. 'What are you going to do with me?' he said.

'I'm glad you asked,' said Dakhil, with a look that made Jamie wish he hadn't. 'You have a starring role in my plan.'

He blew a sparkling wish and two chairs appeared magically behind him. He and Dabir sat down and studied Jamie.

'Mint tea!' ordered Dabir as he made himself comfortable. Balthazar snapped into action and fetched a silver teapot and three small glasses.

'Want some?' asked Dabir, offering a cup to Jamie. 'Or maybe you'd prefer some of that cloud ice cream you're always going on about?'

Dabir scooped some cloud from the ground, blew a sparkling wish of his own and a huge bowl of ice cream appeared in his hands. Dabir offered it to Jamie. The ice cream was chocolate – Jamie's favourite flavour – but he wasn't going to take it from Dabir. He shook his head. 'You think tea and ice cream will make me want to help you?'

'Fair enough!' said Dabir, blowing another shimmering wish. 'Dylan can have it!'

The bowl lifted from Dabir's hands, flew through the air and tipped itself over Dylan's head. Dylan didn't even flinch as the chocolate trickled down his face. Dabir laughed and thumped his chair in delight.

'You big bully!' shouted Jamie.

'Watch your tongue!' said Dabir, and Jamie suddenly found himself enveloped in a cloud of stars. When they evaporated, Jamie's mouth felt strange. He looked down to see that his tongue had been turned into a hissing, spitting rattlesnake!

'Mmmth! Mmmth! Mmmth!' spluttered Jamie, shaking in terror.

'Boys, boys, boys!' cooed Dakhil, blowing out a wish of his own that returned Jamie's tongue to normal. 'There'll be plenty of time for playing later!'

'You asked me what I was going to do with you,' said Dakhil with a coy smile. 'Well, I'm going to use you to betray Methuzular.'

Jamie shook his head. He would never betray his great uncle.

'You may shake your head now,' said Dakhil, 'but I think you'll change your mind. I can be very persuasive. You see, I'm finished with humans, Jamie. For a long time I wanted to wage war against them and punish them for all the hard work they make us genies do without thanks.' Dakhil took a sip of tea and smacked his lips. 'But trapped in that bottle I began to think. I realised that it isn't humans who have been cruellest to my family – it's other genies.'

Dakhil leant forward and warmed to his theme. 'It wasn't humans who ignored my genius – it was genies. And it wasn't humans who banished my son and me to a bottle – it was genies. So now it is genies who are going to pay,' he said. 'The human world has nothing to fear from me any more. I'll shatter all the portals that connect the genie world to the human world, and forget about them. I've already broken the portal that you came through. Humans will get no more wishes, and all that good luck they take for granted will disappear, but that's not so bad, is it? How can they miss something they don't even know exists?'

'But genies are supposed to help humans,' said Jamie. 'It's what they do! They keep watch on the human world, and make our lives easier by spreading good fortune or by helping us out with wishes when we really need them. Humans might not usually notice that it's happening, but that doesn't mean it isn't important! Most genies love helping humans, it's why they spend so long training at the Genie Academy, for goodness' sake! Why would they even bother going if they didn't want to help? You plan to change the genie way of life for ever, but what if they don't want it to change?'

'Thanks to my hypno-wish they'll have no choice in the matter!' said Dakhil, his eyes glowering darkly. 'But we have to act quickly. Dabir and I are going to hypnotise every genie in the Academy, teach them the hypno-wish and use them to hypnotise every genie in Lampville before they even guess what's happening! Before long every genie in the world will be under my power!'

Dakhil stood and began to strut around the cavern. 'Just imagine it, Jamie! I will be the most powerful genie in the world! Dabir and I will live like kings and genie after genie will do our bidding!'

Dakhil stopped his boasting and looked at Jamie. 'The mighty Methuzular will be the first to

transformed. He will become nothing more than my genie butler! Methuzular, clip my toenails! Methuzular, make my dinner! Methuzular, be my foot rest!' Dakhil slumped back into his chair and mimed placing his feet upon a crouching Methuzular with a satisfied smile.

Dabir giggled and clapped in delight.

'This is where you come in, Jamie,' said Dakhil, suddenly serious. 'Dabir and I are preparing a little ambush for Methuzular. You are going to bring him to us. We must put him under the hypno-wish first. He is the most powerful genie in Lampville, after me of course, and when the wish worms its way into his ear he will do whatever I say! He'll give me the Book of Wishes, hypnotise his own students and lead them into Lampville to hypnotise everybody else! With him on our side, we will be unstoppable! You just need to bring him here and we will do the rest.'

Jamie suddenly realised what he was being asked to do. 'I'll never betray Methuzular!' he said firmly.

'You are going to bring Methuzular to us,' sneered Dabir. 'He'll listen to you. Bring him here and we will trap him and hypnotise him and turn him on his students.'

'So you keep saying,' said Jamie, 'but why would I do something like that? I would rather die than betray Methuzular.'

'I know that,' said Dakhil, peering through the bars, 'but if you don't do as I say, your best friend Dylan Reid will die instead!'

CHAPTER 5

Dabir scurried to the back of the cavern and returned dragging two heavy sets of rusty chains and clamped them around the motionless Dylan.

'He's such a good boy,' cooed Dakhil, stroking Dylan's cheek with a bony finger. 'Always does what he's told! You'd do well to learn from him, Jamie Najar.'

Jamie felt rage churning inside him, but there was nothing he could do.

When Dabir had finished, Dakhil produced three large padlocks and secured the chains, locking them in place with a key that swung from a chain dangling from his waistcoat. 'We thought about hypnotising you and then ordering you to betray Methuzular,' said Dakhil, 'but as you noticed, hypnotism sometimes makes people behave a little strangely. Methuzular would have

smelt a rat much quicker than you did.'

'So we had to think of something else,' said Dabir with a slimy grin. Dakhil blew a sparkling wish at

Dylan and the boy floated into the air. His chains clanked as he swept past the cage and up towards the ceiling. Jamie craned his neck to watch and soon Dylan was wedged against the cavern roof.

'Dylan is going to stay there until you return with Methuzular,' said Dakhil. 'Tell Methuzular you have secret, urgent business and he must follow you. Balthazar will go with you to make sure you don't try and warn him along the way. And just to make extra sure you *do* return . . .'

Dakhil blew out a wish and the ground began to shake violently. Jamie clung to the cage bars just to be able to stay on his feet. For a moment he thought that the stalactites hanging from the cavern ceiling were going to be shaken loose and plunge to the floor like deadly spears, but instead sharp silver spikes rose from the floor. They grew steadily until they were as tall as Jamie and then they stopped, glinting in the flickering torchlight.

Dabir touched the tip of one of the spikes. 'These skewers are razor sharp,' he explained with a smile. 'They will continue to grow until you return with Methuzular. If you don't come back,

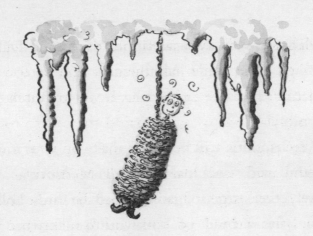

or if you take too long, poor Dylan will be turned into a human kebab!'

Jamie looked in horror as he realised that the spikes were positioned directly beneath his chained friend.

'That is your choice, Jamie Najar,' said Dakhil with a sinister smile. 'Methuzular or Dylan.'

Jamie's mind began to race. It was an impossible decision.

'Perhaps this will help you make up your mind,' Dakhil said, clicking his fingers. Slowly, very slowly, the spikes began to inch towards Dylan. Jamie felt a bead of sweat trickle between his shoulder blades and he shuddered. The nasty genie produced a key from around his neck and unlocked the cage.

The barred door creaked open and Dakhil beckoned Jamie forward. 'Bring me Methuzular,' he said, pointing towards a gloomy tunnel, 'and then you and Dylan can go home. The human world will be perfectly safe. It's only the genies who need to worry — and why should you care about them?'

Jamie looked into the scheming genie's cold black eyes and felt anger bubbling inside. 'Because I love the genie world!' he wanted to shout. 'Because I believe that true genies should follow the genie motto to live lightly and shine brightly.

Genies as selfish as you and your son should be banished for ever!'

But Jamie stopped himself. The spikes were slowly creeping towards his trapped best friend. Blinking back tears of frustration, he looked at Dakhil. 'OK,' he said in a quiet, faltering voice. 'I'll do it.'

Dakhil cupped a sarcastic hand round his ear. 'I beg your pardon, Jamie? I didn't quite catch that.'

'I said I'll bring you Methuzular,' said Jamie, stepping out of the cage. 'Just don't hurt Dylan.'

'What happens to Dylan is up to you,' said Dakhil with a grin. 'So you'd better be quick!'

Dakhil snapped his fingers and Balthazar came over. 'I have taught Balthazar a safe route through the tunnels to the Academy,' explained Dakhil. 'But beware – these tunnels are long and maze-like and many are filled with wish traps. I advise you to stay by his side. Should you get lost on your journey then you may be killed, and even if you are not, you will never return in time to save Dylan.'

Jamie gulped. He didn't even want to think about it.

Dakhil turned to Balthazar. 'Take Jamie to Methuzular's office in the Academy,' he boomed. 'Make sure he asks Methuzular to accompany him here. If you hear him say anything else, or warn anyone, you must stop him! Stay close to him, and lead them straight back.'

'Yes, master,' said Balthazar, giving Dakhil a solemn nod. Dabir snatched two flaming torches from a pair of holders and

pointed to one of the tunnels that led away from the cavern.

'The Academy is that way,' he said. 'Good luck.'

Jamie and Balthazar took a torch each, a cool

breeze ruffling their hair as they peered into the darkness.

'Be quick, Jamie,' warned Dakhil. 'Dylan doesn't have long until he's turned into a human pin cushion!'

Dakhil and Dabir's cackles filled the cavern, but before Jamie could say a word, Balthazar had grabbed his hand and pulled him into the tunnel.

CHAPTER 6

Jamie and Balthazar's footsteps echoed all around as they crunched on the crumbly cloud ground.

'Stay close,' hissed Balthazar as he pulled Jamie along.

Jamie did as he was told, although it was weird to both be with his friend and feel like he was with a total stranger at the same time.

The flickering torches cast strange shadows on the tunnel wall. Jamie tried not to think about all

the spiders
and creepy
crawlies
lurking in
the gloom.
He knew
they were
the least of
his worries –
but he still
didn't want
to come face
to tentacle
with them.

'Balthazar,'
hissed Jamie,
when they were far enough away from the cavern
for Dakhil not to hear. 'Don't do this. You're my
friend. You have to remember that?'

Balthazar didn't even break step but just yanked
Jamie further along the tunnel.

'What about the teapot and the Formula One
race?' pleaded Jamie.

Jamie had first met Balthazar when he had accidentally released him from a battered old teapot his gran had given him for a birthday present. The Formula One race was the first wish Balthazar had granted for Jamie.

But if Balthazar remembered, he didn't show it. He just continued to guide Jamie past cobwebbed clouds and damp, dark puddles.

Jamie began to consider how he could foil

Dakhil's plan. He couldn't lure Methuzular directly into Dakhil's trap. Methuzular had done so much for him that the thought of tricking him made Jamie shudder, plus he didn't want to be the one who helped turn every genie in Lampville into a slave. But at the same time Jamie couldn't let Dylan be skewered! How would he explain that to Dylan's parents? 'I'm sorry, Mr and Mrs Reid. Your son is now a kebab. Would you like chilli sauce with that?'

Jamie told himself to think positively. Right now it was just him and Balthazar. It was one on one. Dakhil and Dabir were far enough away not to be a threat. He should take a chance while it was just the two of them, he thought. Who knew if he'd get another opportunity like this? Balthazar could be pretty clumsy – Jamie might just be able to overpower him and find a way back to Dakhil's cavern to rescue Dylan. Then the two of them could race to the Academy and raise the alarm. Dylan would still be hypnotised but Jamie was sure he could get him to follow him somehow. He owed it to Dylan, Balthazar and Methuzular to at least try!

They had come to a fork in the tunnel. Somewhere above them water was dripping. Jamie thought the rock formation by the right hand tunnel looked like a face with a long pointy nose.

As Balthazar paused, checking which way to go, Jamie decided to seize the moment. 'Sorry,' he muttered under his breath, as Balthazar began to lead him left, and he stamped down hard on Balthazar's foot.

The genie's howls filled the tunnel. Balthazar

let go of Jamie and clutched his throbbing foot with both hands, hopping up and down. Jamie pushed the unbalanced genie over and Balthazar clattered onto the floor like a genie-shaped skittle. It was the chance Jamie needed. He doubled back and raced into the right-hand tunnel. Behind him Jamie heard Balthazar roar as he clambered to his feet.

Jamie dodged around a corner and took a sharp left into an adjacent tunnel, hoping to go full circle and head back towards the cavern. He could hear Balthazar's limping footsteps giving slow and painful chase. Jamie ran forward, the flaming torch doing little to light his way. He ducked left and right, down tunnels and through cracks. With his sore foot, Balthazar had no chance of keeping up and soon Jamie was alone.

He stopped to catch his breath and he noticed a strange shape in the tunnel ahead. He crept closer and could barely contain his amazement. There, in front of him, was a wicker basket. That

was weird, even for Lampville! Who'd have a picnic down here? Forget teddy bears' picnic, this would be a teddy scares picnic!

As Jamie bent down to examine it, the lid suddenly flew off and sparkling smoke filled the air. Jamie's heart began to beat quickly. It was a wish cloud – anything could happen!

When the cloud evaporated, Jamie was surprised to find a frog sitting on the ground by the basket. That was it. Just a frog.

Jamie smiled, and calmed down. He was about to give the frog a pat when it opened its mouth and let out a huge 'RIBBIT!'

Fire shot across the tunnel from the frog's

mouth like a flame-thrower. Startled, Jamie pulled his burnt fingers out of the way.

Of course! This must be one of the wish traps that Dakhil had warned him about! He'd forgotten all about them. Jamie cursed himself. How could he have been so stupid to run away from Balthazar when he needed him to show him the safe way through the tunnels?

The frog hopped closer and, with a massive leap, jumped onto Jamie's shoulder. The frog opened its mouth to ribbit once again. It was going to breathe fire right into Jamie's face! Jamie frantically brushed the frog away. As it tumbled to the ground, it released its flames, catching Jamie's shoes. Suddenly his feet were ablaze. Like a demented disco dancer, Jamie stamped out the fire. He had to get away before the frog turned him into a crisp! Jamie clutched the torch and ran. He could hear the frog as it hopped after him, and feel the heat roll towards him as it lit up the tunnel with each new croak. He risked a glance behind him as the croaks grew fainter, but tumbled into another wicker basket lurking in the half-light as he did,

setting off a second sparkling wish cloud.
Arrows shot out from the basket
and thudded into the wall
behind him. Jamie leapt
into a judo roll as a
second volley
flew through
the air and just
missed his feet.
He silently
thanked Josh
and Will for teaching it to him, though he bet
they'd never had to use it like that before!

As Jamie ran on, a new wish trap seemed to be
waiting for him in every tunnel. It seemed that
wherever he turned, Dakhil had
another trap lying in
store. He ducked giant
rolling rocks,
hurdled a
barbed trip wire
and swung
across a pool of

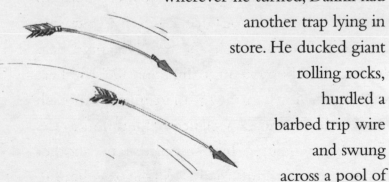

alligators that suddenly appeared snapping in his path. He leant against the tunnel wall, trying to catch his breath. He couldn't go on like this! Even if he managed to avoid all the wish traps and get back to the cavern, he'd be too exhausted to save Dylan, and he was losing precious time.

He was hopelessly lost now, and could only groan when he spotted yet another wish trap in the distance. He tried to sneak carefully past, but even the tiniest footsteps seemed to spring the traps. The sparkling cloud billowed from the basket and Jamie watched in terror as it evaporated to reveal a pack of hissing snakes. That would have been bad enough, but a moment later, they sprouted wings and hurled themselves right at him.

Still clutching the torch, he sprinted as fast as he could. He stole a glance over his shoulder and saw the snapping jaws of the biggest flying snake right behind him, its fangs dripping with venom. Jamie ducked into a smaller tunnel in a desperate attempt to shake them off but the snakes seemed able to track him like scaly heat-seeking missiles.

Suddenly he screeched to a halt. Up ahead was something even worse than a wish trap – it was a dead end. There was nowhere left to run.

Jamie turned to face the snakes, backing up against the wall. He swung the torch like a club, desperately trying to frighten the snakes away. For a moment it worked, but he swung it so hard that the flame streamed and then went out. Jamie felt his heart sink as the tunnel was plunged into darkness. He desperately tried to think of a wish that he could use – but he knew very few wishes off by heart, and he even if he could remember one that would help, his mind was in such a whirl that the chances of concentrating hard enough to make one seemed remote. He closed his eyes and waited for the first snake's fangs to pierce his flesh.

Suddenly the tunnel was filled with heat. Jamie opened his eyes to see the snakes writhing in a massive fireball. He shielded his face from the flames, and as they died away, a figure emerged from the smoke and stepped over the dying snakes. Jamie couldn't believe it. It was Balthazar! His friend had saved his life! That's what it had taken to break Balthazar out of being hypnotised.

Jamie had never been so happy to see him as

Balthazar reached out . . . and grabbed Jamie by the scruff of his neck.

'My orders were to stay close to you!' hissed the still hypnotised Balthazar, hoisting Jamie over his shoulder.

Exhausted, Jamie closed his eyes as Balthazar started to carry him over the blackened bodies of the dead flying snakes.

His dangerous escape had been for nothing.

CHAPTER 7

When Jamie opened his eyes, he was very confused by what he saw. Eventually he realised he was looking at Balthazar's bottom wobbling to and fro. But he could see it very clearly. Too clearly, in fact.

He looked round and saw sunlight streaming through an opening just up ahead. As they got closer, Jamie saw that the opening was covered with thick, leafy branches. Carefully, Balthazar moved the branches to one side and threw Jamie down to the ground outside of the tunnel. Then Balthazar replaced the branches, hiding the opening from anyone who didn't know it was there.

Jamie took deep lungfuls of fresh air as his eyes adjusted to the glare of the sun. Even though he had only been in the tunnels for a short time, he had feared he might never see daylight again. Jamie glanced around him and recognised the main Genie Academy building towering over cloud trees in the distance, and the tumble-down Alim Tower behind it. Between Jamie and the Academy were beautiful playing fields and the Academy's magnificent magic carpet racing track. Jamie had spent a lot of time there when he had been at the Academy. Magic carpet racing had been one of his favourite things to do!

Jamie tried to remember the location of the tunnel entrance in case he got another chance to escape. But his heart sank as he realised that even if he found the entrance, there was no way he would find his way back to Dylan and the cavern. He'd have to think of something else.

'Let's get moving,' grunted Balthazar in his dreamy, faraway voice.

Jamie picked himself up and walked with Balthazar past the ornate topiary hedges trimmed into hundreds of shapes, from lamps to flying carpets, dragons to shooting stars. In the distance, the Academy looked majestic. Jamie remembered the many happy times he had shared with his friends in its classrooms and dormitories. Part of him wanted to shake loose of Balthazar and go and say hello to all the teachers and genies he loved and missed so dearly, but the thought that all that was magical about the Academy and the genie way of life could be destroyed if Dakhil and Dabir got their way kept him close.

As they hurried on, Jamie tried to figure out a new plan. He reckoned the only way he could be sure of saving Dylan was to get Methuzular to come with him into the tunnels. But Jamie had to find a way to warn Methuzular what was going on so at least he'd be prepared for Dakhil and Dabir.

The trouble was going to be Balthazar.

They were crossing the magic carpet track when a familiar voice rang out. 'Jamie Najar? Is that you?'

Jamie turned to see Adeel Maloof, his best friend when he had been studying at the Academy, running across the paddock with his magic carpets, Sunray and Threadbare, floating just behind.

'Remember to stick to Dakhil's plan,' warned Balthazar quietly.

'Adeel!' called Jamie, with a friendly wave. 'It's nice to see you!'

Threadbare, Jamie's favourite carpet, overtook Adeel and covered Jamie in a clothy cuddle. Jamie tickled its tassels.

'What are you doing here, Jamie? asked Adeel. 'Has Methuzular summoned you?'

Jamie shook his head.

'It's a surprise visit,' he half-lied. 'Balthazar needed my help, isn't that right, Balthazar?'

Balthazar nodded.

'And you weren't going to say hello?' exclaimed Adeel. 'The cheek of it!' Adeel gave Jamie a playful dig in the ribs. 'I haven't seen you for ages. I've got a new joke for you! What has two arms, two legs and flies like a loony?'

James shrugged his shoulders. He didn't know.

'You!' said Adeel, blowing out a sparkling wish. Jamie felt a strange tickling sensation between his shoulder blades. Before he knew what was happening, two wings had sprouted from his back

and he was flying into the air.

Adeel giggled and clapped his hands in delight. Jamie flapped his arms like a startled starling. Below him Adeel was rolling on the ground, tears of laughter streaming down his face. Despite himself Jamie smiled. It was always a pleasure to see his kind-hearted, blond haired, best genie friend enjoying himself.

'Come on! Get your own back! See if you can

remember any of the wishes I taught you!' Adeel said as the wish dissolved and Jamie landed on the ground with a bump.

Before Jamie had chance to dream up a wishy revenge, Balthazar sprung into action. 'We've no time for this!' he said.

Adeel fixed Balthazar with an angry stare. 'Who yanked your tassels, grumpy drawers?' he said. 'We were only having a bit of fun.'

'Sorry, Adeel,' said Jamie, remembering the situation they were in. 'Balthazar's right, we are in a bit of a rush. Give me a welcome back hug and I'll see you later.'

As Adeel clung to Jamie, Jamie thought quickly and whispered into his ear. 'I need your help! Balthazar's hypnotised. Everyone's in danger. Meet me in Methuzular's office in fifteen minutes and I'll explain everything!'

Jamie knew that he needed as many people he could trust on his side as possible and he didn't trust anyone more than Adeel.

Jamie pulled away and Adeel gave him a curious look. Jamie

could tell Adeel was trying to work out if this was some kind of joke.

'Lovely to see you!' said Jamie loudly. 'Can't talk — we really are in a hurry, aren't we, Balthazar?'

Balthazar nodded, took Jamie's arm and led him into the school.

They went through the main doors of the Academy and Balthazar led Jamie down the corridor. As they walked, Jamie spotted trainee genies hard at work in some of the classrooms. Through the doors he saw a genie practising juggling fire and through another a group of genies were trying to catch a chair that was hurtling around the room. Balthazar pulled Jamie past the dinner hall and down a smaller corridor. School photos hung from the wall and a cabinet filled with magic carpet trophies stood on one side.

The trainee genies moved out of the way when they saw the determined look on Balthazar's face. Jamie waved to one or two familiar faces as he passed, but there was no way Balthazar was letting him stop to say hello.

Soon they were outside the headmaster's office. Jamie knocked and they went inside. Methuzular was sitting behind his desk wearing golden robes. He was opening his post with an ornate letter knife. He looked up to see who had entered his office and his bushy eyebrows nearly flew off his forehead in surprise when he saw Jamie looking back at him.

'Jamie Najar!' he spluttered, his grey eyes

twinkling with delight. 'What are you doing here?'

Jamie took a step into the room as Balthazar guarded the door. 'I need to speak to you!' he said.

Balthazar shot Jamie a warning look as Methuzular stood and held him close for a hug. The kindly headmaster pulled away before Jamie had a chance to whisper anything to him.

'This is most unexpected, Jamie,' said Methuzular. 'You should have told me you were coming and I'd have prepared a welcome. How is that sister of mine?'

Aware Balthazar was listening to every word, Jamie took a deep breath, and did as he'd been told.

'We've no time for that,' he said, moving round the desk so that he was between Balthazar and Methuzular. 'You've got to come with us to the caverns underneath the school. Something terrible is happening that you have to see for yourself!'

As he spoke, Jamie positioned himself so that the hypnotised genie couldn't see his hands. While he told Methuzlar what Balthazar wanted to hear Jamie scrawled, unseen, on Methuzular's homework register with a gold fountain pen.

Methuzular looked deep into Jamie's eyes and could tell instantly that the young boy was being deadly serious.

'Balthazar?' he mouthed silently.

Jamie gave the slightest of nods and before he knew what was happening, Methuzlar had leapt over the desk, pushed Jamie to one side and knocked Balthazar to the floor.

'Quick,' said Methuzular, grabbing Jamie and pulling him towards the bookcase. 'In situations like this the element of surprise is all important. Speaking of which . . .'

The headmaster counted three books across on the second shelf from the top and pulled out a thick blue book. Behind them Balthazar was pulling himself to his feet.

'Methuzular!' warned Jamie.

There was a loud click, and the bookcase swung open to reveal a secret room. In the same moment,

Methuzular shoved Jamie inside, closing the door on Balthazar's outstretched fingers.

Jamie heard the hypnotised genie yowl, and then start pounding angrily on the other side of the bookcase door. They were standing in a small cupboard-sized room with a desk and a chair. On the desk lay the Book of Wishes.

'Don't worry,' said Methuzlar. 'He won't get in! Tell me what's happened.'

'It's a trap! Dakhil and Dabir are plotting in the caverns beneath the Academy and need you —'

'Hold your horses, Jamie,' said Methuzular gently. 'Dakhil's been released? And Dabir? They're in the caverns under the Academy?' He staggered in shock and collapsed into the chair.

'That's not all,' continued Jamie. 'They've hypnotised Balthazar and my best friend, Dylan.'

Methuzular held up his hands for quiet. 'Start at the beginning, Jamie,' he said. 'Leave nothing out.'

Remembering that he didn't have long to be back in time to rescue Dylan, Jamie quickly explained about the mistake with the bottle and the hypno-wish. Then he told Methuzular all about Dakhil's plans. By the time Jamie had finished, all the colour had drained from Methuzular's face.

Outside, Balthazar had stopped his banging.

'Do you think he's gone?' asked Jamie.

Methuzular nodded. 'He'll have gone to get help.'

Jamie gulped. 'We need to stop him! If he tells Dakhil what I've done, Dylan will be minced meat – literally!'

'Don't worry, Jamie. We'll fix this!' Methuzular whispered, pushing open the bookcase door. 'It is a dangerous and long-lasting wish though. Until it is reversed, no other wish will work on those that are hypnotised. But Dabir and Dakhil are still vulnerable, and no match for my powers!'

For just a moment, Jamie was sure everything was going to be all right – until they stepped into Methuzular's office and found that Balthazar Najar hadn't gone for help. He was waiting silently for them, the ornate letter knife in his hands.

CHAPTER 8

Jamie and Methuzular stood in the bookcase doorway while Balthazar glared at them.

'You tried to trick me,' he said in his dreamy, faraway voice, waving the sharp knife to and fro. 'You tried to get away from me. Again!'

Methuzular took a step forwards. 'Put down the knife, Balthazar,' he said.

Balthazar swiped the letter knife in a vicious arc and Methuzular jumped out of the way, clattering into a pair of golden candlesticks that stood by his door.

'He won't listen to you,' said Jamie. 'He only obeys Dakhil and Dabir.'

Methuzular picked himself up and Balthazar lunged again. Jamie pulled the headmaster clear of the flashing blade.

'We have to stop him,' said Methuzular. 'I will try my best to do so without hurting him. Wishes won't work on him while he's hypnotised, but they will work on everything else!' Methuzular blew a wish cloud at the floor. As Balthazar lashed out at Jamie with the knife, hundreds of marbles emerged from the cloud and littered the floor. Balthazar's feet scrambled wildly on their slippery surfaces for a second before he tumbled onto his back.

Jamie seized his chance and made a grab for the knife. Balthazar wasn't as dazed as he appeared and gripped Jamie's wrist, pulling him down on top of him. There was a scuffle and

when Balthazar got to his feet, he had Jamie held
like a human shield between himself and
Methuzular. Jamie froze, the blade of the knife
pressing against his neck.

Methuzular danced around his office trying to
get a clear shot for one of his wishes, but it was no
use. 'I can't risk it, Jamie,' said Methuzular. 'Any
wish I make might affect you by mistake.'

Balthazar grinned. This was just what he wanted. He backed towards the office door, dragging Jamie with him.

'You'll never get away with it!' warned Methuzular.

But the zombie-like genie didn't care. He fumbled for the door handle. Balthazar was going to take Jamie back to Dakhil and Dabir where Jamie was sure he'd join Dylan on the roof of the cavern, if Dylan wasn't already dead, of course. Jamie knew Methuzular would try and rescue them both, which would bring him to the cavern anyway, just as Dakhil had planned.

The pair were shuffling towards the corridor like a couple of nervous ballroom dancers when Jamie heard a loud *whoosh*, a vicious *clang* and suddenly Balthazar's grip went limp as the knife fell to the floor. Balthazar crumpled in a heap and Jamie turned to see what had happened.

Adeel stood in the doorway, holding one of Methuzular's golden candlesticks. Jamie had never been more relieved to see his friend in all his life. Balthazar lay collapsed on Methuzular's office rug.

'What on Earth is going on?' asked Adeel, putting the candlestick back in its place. 'Has Balthazar gone mad?'

'Worse,' said Methuzular, rushing to Jamie's side. 'Are you all right?'

Jamie nodded, but crouched down to check on Balthazar.

'He'll be fine,' said Methuzular, pulling Balthazar into his chair. 'But he'll come round soon. We must be ready. I know the reverse hypno-wish, but it is extremely difficult – very few genies have enough power and experience to cast it. It means pitching your magic against another genie's magic and using your skills to overpower them. I would need time to gather the strength, and I believe time is something we don't have enough of right now.'

Jamie nodded. They needed to get back to save Dylan.

Methuzular blew a shimmering wish at the chair and ropes appeared from the arms of the chair, binding Balthazar tight.

'This should keep him out of trouble for now,' said Methuzular.

When Balthazar was safely secured, Jamie and Methuzular took it in turns to tell Adeel all about Dakhil, Dabir and their terrible plan.

As they finished, Balthazar began to cough and splutter and his eyes opened.

'Why does my head feel like it's been sat on by an elephant?' he said. Then he saw that he was tied to Methuzular's chair. 'And what's going on here? I mean, I like sitting as much as the next genie, but I don't have to be forced into it!'

A smile began to play across Jamie's lips. That didn't sound like the hypnotised Balthazar he'd been hearing recently, that sounded like the old Balthazar he knew and loved.

'Balthazar!' exclaimed Jamie. 'You're back!'

'Am I?' said Balthazar with a confused smile. 'Where have I been?'

Methuzular looked at Balthazar in amazement. 'That clout Adeel gave Balthazar with the candlestick has obviously achieved what only a very powerful reversal spell can usually achieve. It has brought Balthazar back to his senses and rid his mind of the hypno-wish altogether. Although he is lucky not to have been seriously hurt.'

When they were certain it was safe, Methuzular wished away the ropes and Balthazar rose to his feet.

'Uh-oh!' he said, tumbling into the desk and sending Methuzular's diary flying. 'I feel dizzy. And why am I hatching an egg on my head?' he spluttered, feeling the large lump that had been left there by Adeel. Balthazar collapsed

into the chair and knocked over
Methuzular's inkpot.

'Looks like he's back
to his clumsy best,' said
Jamie with a grin.

'Unfortunately,'
sighed
Methuzular,
dabbing at
the ink
spreading
across his desk, but
he was smiling as he said it.

As quickly as he could, Jamie told Balthazar all
that had happened. With each new revelation,
Balthazar got more and more upset.

'You mean I set Dakhil and Dabir free?' he
wailed, tears pouring down his face. 'The Genie
Congress are going to banish me for ever for this!'

The Genie Congress was made up of the wisest
genies in all of Lampville. They ruled over the
other genies and decided on punishments when
they were necessary.

Methuzular placed a calming hand on Balthazar's shoulder. 'I will put in a good word,' promised the kindly headmaster. 'Besides, if you help us capture Dakhil and Dabir, then you will have fixed what you broke and all will be well.'

'What are we going to do?' asked Adeel.

Methuzular rose to his feet. 'The only thing we can do. If it's Methuzular they want,' he said, 'then it's Methuzular they are going to get!'

CHAPTER 9

Methuzular snatched his cloak from the stand and hurried into the corridor.

'Follow me,' he said, 'and bring those candlesticks. I could cast a light wish or two, but they do take it out of me and I want to be full of energy when I face Dakhil and Dabir – who knows what they have in mind.'

Adeel and Jamie grabbed a candlestick each while the half-dazed Balthazar stumbled behind them.

As they strode past the dinner hall, Jamie could see all the genies inside scooping up clouds and transforming them into delicious plates of food with their wishes. Tempting smells filled the air and Jamie licked his lips as a small genie in a green waistcoat wished up a massive pepperoni pizza that was bigger than his face. Jamie wondered how he was ever going to fit it in his mouth! In that moment Jamie truly appreciated how wonderful the genie world was and how important it was that he and his friends preserved it for evermore.

As they left the bustle of the dinner hall behind them, Methuzular began to explain his idea. 'We are going to pretend that their plan worked,' he said. 'They'll think Balthazar is still on their side and that I have willingly accompanied you, without knowing what is really happening. Dakhil and Dabir won't expect me to be ready for them, nor that Balthazar isn't obeying their commands any more! They'll free Dylan and then Balthazar and I will tackle Dabir and Dakhil.'

'What about me?' asked Jamie.

'You and Dylan run for your lives,' said Methuzular, barging through the large doors at the front of the Academy. 'It's vital you get back home. Run to the Portal of Dreams in Farah Najar's classroom and use it.'

Jamie remembered Farah — she was the teacher who had first shown him how to use the portal. It was kept in her classroom for the whole school to practise with.

Methuzular stopped by a cloud tree and faced Jamie. 'That is the most important thing,' he said, fixing him with a fierce stare. 'We don't know what Dakhil and Dabir have in store for us. No matter what happens, you need to get away. You may be tempted to stop and help. You mustn't do that, no matter what you see. It is vital that you and Dylan return home. Do you understand?'

Jamie nodded. If Dylan and he weren't back by the morning, he knew what a difficult position it would put his gran in. How could she explain to his parents, let alone the police, about the genie world? They'd think she was battier than a bat who's just got out of bat school and has discovered they really like cricket.

'Which way to the tunnel entrance?' asked Methuzular.

Jamie pointed across the playing fields and Methuzular, Adeel and Balthazar followed him to the tunnel opening.

'As I said before, the element of surprise is very important in situations like this,' explained Methuzular as they walked. 'Dakhil and Dabir can't get suspicious. They need to believe Balthazar is still under their control and that I know nothing.'

Balthazar nodded.

'You need to pretend to be hypnotised,' said Jamie. 'Act like you were before Adeel hit you.'

Balthazar bit his lip and shook his head. 'I don't remember how I was,' he said quietly.

'You were like a zombie,' explained Jamie.

'What? Like this?' asked Balthazar, sticking out his arms. 'Mmm, brains!'

Despite himself, Jamie laughed. 'No! It was more dreamy than that!' he explained, doing an impression of how distant Balthazar had been. 'I am your servant, Dakhil. Yes, master.'

'I'm sure I'd never have said that,' said Balthazar.

'You did!' insisted Jamie. 'And your eyes had a faraway look, like you were day-dreaming or something.'

'How on earth am I going to do that?' asked Balthazar as the group made their way past the magic carpet track.

'Try doing a really difficult sum in your head,' Adeel said. 'Something impossible, like the square root of 4,534,323! Maths always puts me in a daze!'

Balthazar nearly choked. 'I'll never work that out!'

'You don't have to,' explained Adeel, 'but while your brain tries to work it out, your eyes will glaze over and you'll look just like you did before.'

Sure enough, as Balthazar tried to work out the sum, his eyes became glassy and gained their previous distant look.

'That's perfect!' laughed Jamie. 'Just try not to count on your fingers at the same time!'

They reached the edge of the magic carpet track and Jamie guided them to the covered entrance. Together they pulled away the branches and peered into the darkness.

Instantly, candles appeared in their holders and

burst into flame. Jamie jumped, but Methuzular just smiled. 'Self-lighting candles,' he told him. 'Essential for working late when your caretaker keeps moving your matches.' Methuzular took the candle Adeel was holding and passed it to Balthazar.

'Hey,' said Adeel. 'What about me?'

'You are waiting here,' said Methuzular.

'What!' said Adeel. 'I have to come! I want to give Dabir a piece of my mind, and I could help you all.'

Methuzular placed his hand on Adeel's shoulder. 'You have an even more important job to do. We four are the only ones who know what Dabir and Dakhil are up to. What if anything happens to us? I want you to take the Book of Wishes to a safe place.'

Methuzular told Adeel how to open the secret bookcase door to the room where it was kept.

'We all know the location of the Book of

Wishes,' he said, looking at Balthazar and Jamie. 'If something goes wrong, Dakhil and Dabir may force us to tell them where it is hidden. If we don't know, we can't tell them. If they manage to trap us, it's only the Book of Wishes that will save us.' He turned to Adeel. 'Keep it safe until I ask for it once again. It contains the hypno-wish reversal wish. There is still a chance, should things go badly wrong, that you might be able to save the genie world without us.'

Adeel gulped as the magnitude of what Methuzular was saying sunk in. He was being trusted with a very important job.

'Very well, Methuzular,' said Adeel. 'But I hope it doesn't come to that.'

Adeel gave Jamie, Balthazar and Methuzular a hug and watched them grip their candlesticks and disappear into the tunnel.

At first there was only one way they could go, but soon they reached a fork in the tunnel.

Jamie turned to Balthazar. 'Which way?' he asked.

Balthahzar scratched his head and peered down

the left and right openings in turn. 'I don't know,' he admitted.

'But Dakhil told you the safe tunnels to take!' said Jamie.

'That must have been when I was hypnotised,' explained Balthazar. 'I told you, I don't remember anything about when they put the hypno-wish on me.'

Jamie stamped his foot in frustration. There was no way he could remember either – he had been too exhausted after the chase to keep his eyes open.

'If Dakhil's cavern is under the Academy then

we want the tunnel that leads in that direction,' said Methuzular. 'The Academy is off to our right, so let's take that one.'

Methuzular nodded towards the right-hand tunnel and Jamie and Balthazar guided the way with their candles. They tried to keep the direction of the Academy in their minds and chose tunnels that seemed to lead in the right direction but soon even the mighty Methuzular was lost in the dark shadows.

'Which way now? All the tunnels look the same,' said Balthazar.

'Haven't we been this way before?' asked Jamie.

Suddenly Balthazar spotted something on the ground ahead of them. 'What's this?' he asked, stepping forward to have a closer look.

Jamie froze. 'Don't touch that!' he shouted. But it was too late. A fireball erupted from the wish trap and zoomed towards them. Methuzular, Balthazar and Jamie ducked to the ground. The fireball zoomed over their heads and crashed into the tunnel wall.

'What was that?' said Balthazar.

'A wish trap,'
explained Jamie. 'I
should have
thought to
warn you.
When you
stray from the
safe path to the
cavern, the
tunnels are full of them.'

The basket was quivering again.

'Here comes another one!' warned Jamie. 'Run!'

They got up and dodged around a
corner as the fireball slammed into the
wall, inches from their heads.

'I've never seen anything like
this before,' said Methuzular,
staring at his singed turban.
'Dakhil and Dabir are very
powerful genies. We must not
underestimate them. It will be
hard to defeat them.'

When the next fireball

had erupted, they seized their moment and Jamie and Balthazar pulled Methuzular further down the tunnel. As they ran, Jamie spotted a strange-looking rock.

It looked a bit like a face with a long nose. Jamie smiled. He knew where they were! The cavern lay straight ahead.

'Showtime!' he told them. 'Pretend to be hypnotised, Balthazar,' he instructed. 'We're nearly there!'

Methuzular gave them both a reassuring smile. 'Don't worry,' he said quietly. 'It will all be fine.'

However, something in Methuzular's voice made Jamie realise the headmaster wasn't so sure.

They walked on and soon found themselves entering the central cavern. Dabir and Dakhil turned to look when they heard their footsteps. As soon as they saw Methuzular, they grinned from ear to ear.

'Surprise!' cackled Dabir, rubbing his hands together in delight.

'You!' Methuzular spluttered in fake surprise. 'But how?'

Before Methuzular had time to move, Dakhil sprang into action.

'Seize him,' he commanded, and Balthazar, keen to keep up the pretence, did as he was told, pinning Methuzular's arms to his sides. Methuzular struggled, but it was no use – Balthazar was younger and stronger than him.

'We heard explosions,' Dakhil said, turning to Balthazar. 'What was going on?'

'Wish trap, sir,' mumbled Balthazar in his best faraway voice.

Dakhil's eyes narrowed in suspicion. 'Why were *you* setting off wish traps?' asked Dakhil. 'You know the safe way through the tunnels.'

Balthazar gulped and began to sweat. 'I-I-I . . .' he stammered.

'I wandered off,' said Jamie quickly. It was crucial that Balthazar didn't give them away. 'I thought I knew the fastest way back, and set off a wish trap. I was worried about Dylan. Look, I've brought you Methuzular. Set Dylan free!'

Jamie could see the spikes pressing into Dylan's cheeks. They didn't have a second to lose.

Dakhil shook his head and smiled. 'Did you really believe me when I said I'd let you go? Neither you nor Dylan will ever see home again!'

Methuzular gave Balthazar a nod. Balthazar understood and secretly released the headmaster's arms.

'You are a devil, Dakhil!' Methuzular bellowed, blowing out a sparkling wish. He grabbed Jamie's candlestick, swinging it at Dabir and Dakhil, forcing them back as he flew into the air on a cloud of stars. Methuzular snatched the still-chained Dylan away from the spikes in the nick of time.

'Did you think we weren't expecting this?' bellowed Dakhil. 'We knew a human like Jamie couldn't be trusted!'

A cage appeared in mid-air, trapping Methuzular

and Dylan. The thundercloud bars fizzed with lightning, and Methuzular's wish cloud sparked, then dissolved as the cage fell to the ground. He was powerless.

'Run!' shouted Methuzular to Jamie and Balthazar. 'You have to get away!'

Jamie didn't want to leave his best friend and great uncle to the mercy of Dakhil Ganim, but before he had chance to argue, Balthazar had grabbed his hand and together they hurtled towards the tunnel.

CHAPTER 10

Jamie and Balthazar ran as fast as they could into the darkness. Jamie hated leaving Dylan and Methuzular trapped in a cage, but he knew that at least Dylan was safe from the spikes and he trusted Methuzular to look after him as best he could.

But his heart plummeted as he heard Dakhil yell, 'After them, Dabir!'

Balthazar was still holding the candle but its thin flame did little to light the black around them. Jamie stole a glance over his shoulder and saw Dabir sprinting towards them, grim-faced and determined. Both Balthazar and Jamie knew that getting back to Adeel and the Book of Wishes was their only hope.

Dabir took his chance and blew a sparkling wish. A huge lion appeared out of the cloud and stalked hungrily towards Jamie and Balthazar.

'We'll never outrun that!' said Balthazar. Dabir had the pair trapped. Suddenly the sound of rushing wind filled the tunnel. Dabir looked up, confused, his hair wafting in the breeze as the tunnel grew brighter.

'Jump on board!' yelled Adeel as he and his magic carpet, Sunray, hurtled around the corner and screeched to a stop. Adeel had tied a flaming torch to Sunray's side, and the lion cowered away from the bright light.

Balthazar and Jamie didn't need to be asked twice. Jamie put his arms around Adeel's waist while Balthazar gripped Sunray's rear tassels.

'Where did you come from?' asked Jamie.

But before Adeel could answer, the lion swiped its paw at them blindly and Sunray twisted hard to swerve out of the way.

'Let's get out of here!' shouted Adeel as he gripped Sunray's tassels. 'Hold on tight!'

Adeel gave the tassels a yank and the magic carpet shot off.

'Sorry I'm late!' said Adeel with a mischievous wink. 'I would have been here earlier but for those strange basket things!'

'They're wish traps,' said Jamie.

'They're lethal!' said Adeel. 'Luckily I was on Sunray. The first one I managed to manoeuvre through and once I knew they were dangerous, I kept close to the cavern roof. That seemed to stop them exploding!'

Balthazar glanced back at a furious Dabir and blew him a raspberry.

Dabir's eyes narrowed, and he breathed out a sparkling wish. The lion turned black, shimmered and flattened, and in a flash was replaced by a black magic carpet with a gold trim. Jamie recognised it as Viper, Dabir's vicious magic carpet.

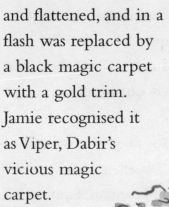

Dabir gave the carpet a kick and it took off in hot pursuit.

Adeel was a fantastic magic carpet rider – he had improved massively since Jamie was last in Lampville – and he steered Sunray skilfully around the twisting tunnels, dodged under stalactites and lurched around tight corners, switching from one tunnel to the next until Jamie began to feel like he was riding the scariest rollercoaster in the world. Jamie pointed up ahead to a low-hanging outcrop of rock and Adeel manoeuvred Sunray down so they were barely skimming the cavern floor. While Dabir was not as good as Adeel, he only had one rider on his carpet, and was keeping up with them every swish of the way.

'How did you find us?' shouted Jamie into Adeel's ear.

'I nearly didn't,' admitted Adeel. 'But there was no way I was going to be left out of an adventure like this,' he explained.

'Methuzular told you to take the Book of Wishes to a safe place,' said Jamie.

'And I have,' said Adeel with a grin, tapping his

waistcoat. 'I wished it smaller and now I'm keeping it with me at all times. It might be heavy and uncomfortable but at least it's safe! And Methuzular didn't say what I had to do *after* I got the book, so I thought I'd come and help!'

Jamie was about to tell Adeel that Methuzular probably wouldn't want him to bring the book into the tunnels when they jumped a boulder and his words were lost, almost like his dinner was!

'Besides,' said Adeel, yanking Sunray left and right, 'you looked like you needed the help.'

Jamie stole a glance over his shoulder at the pursuing genie and had to agree that he was glad Adeel had turned up when he had, even if it put his friend in terrible danger. As he turned back, Jamie saw the rock formation that looked like a face, but they were moving so fast that before he could tell Adeel to take the left-hand tunnel, Adeel had guided Sunray to the right.

'Wrong way!' hissed Jamie.

'Too late!' said Adeel. 'Hold on!'

Balthazar and Jamie clung on for dear life. The right-hand tunnel was not as big as the tunnel that led to the Academy. It hadn't been excavated properly and jagged rocks stuck out from the sides. Adeel dodged left and right doing his best to avoid clattering into them. Jamie's knuckles were white from holding on so tightly, and Balthazar had turned an interesting shade of green.

Jamie could see the wish traps below them, but Adeel was right – zooming over them didn't set them off! Dakhil had clearly thought no one would be crazy enough to try flying a carpet down the tunnels!

Suddenly a lightning bolt shot past them and exploded into the tunnel wall. Jamie looked back. As Dabir steered Viper, he was casting wish after wish, and another bolt shot from his hands.

'Left!' screamed Balthazar, casting his own wishes back, as more lightning bolts hurtled towards them.

Adeel yanked Sunray to the left and the lightning bolt hit the tunnel roof, dislodging a stalactite and sending it plunging into the ground like a guillotine.

'That was close!' shouted Jamie.

'Get us out of here!' yelled Balthazar

'What do you think I'm trying to d—?' said Adeel. His words caught in his throat. 'Oh no!'

Jamie looked. Up ahead, the tunnel was partially blocked by a pile of rubble. 'It's a landslide!' he gasped.

'I think we can make it through,' Adeel said, leaning forward to concentrate.

Jamie's eyes grew wide. There was only a tiny gap at the top of the rocks. There was no way they were going to fit! 'Are you crazy?' he said.

Another lightning bolt shot past his ear. He felt it singe the hair on the top of his head.

'Lightning bolt or landslide?' said Adeel. 'Your choice!'

Jamie lay down as flat as he could and Balthazar did the same. Adeel leant forward into an aerodynamic crouch.

'Hold on tight,' urged Adeel. 'I've never tried this before.'

'Never tried what?' asked Jamie, unsure if he really wanted to know.

Adeel swung Sunray up the side of the tunnel wall, and then spun the carpet like a corkscrew. For a brief moment they were flying upside down on the tunnel roof. Jamie closed his eyes as they swooped between the rubble and the rock ceiling. He felt a sharp stone tear at his clothes as they soared past and then they were through! The

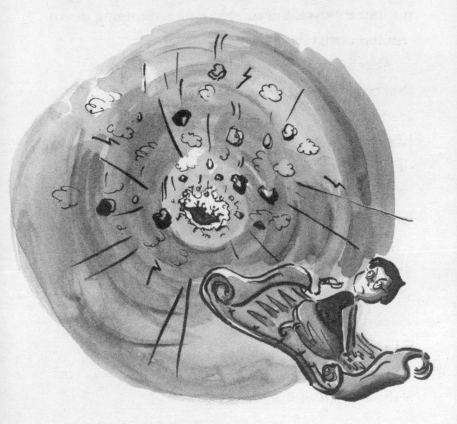

tunnel lit up as another lightning bolt flew through the gap. It smashed into the roof and more rubble tumbled free, creating a rocky avalanche behind them, sealing the gap completely. There was no way for Dabir to get through.

Adeel gently pulled Sunray to a halt and all three of them looked back at the blocked tunnel.

'Nice moves, Adeel!' said Jamie, slumping down on the carpet in relief.

'Yes, brilliant!' said Balthazar. 'Although . . .'

'What?' asked Adeel.

'Well, let's hope this tunnel actually goes somewhere,' said Balthazar, looking at the landslide. 'Otherwise, we're as stuck as a stick insect on a very sticky jam sandwich!'

CHAPTER 11

It was obvious that the tunnel hadn't been used in a long time. It smelt damp and musty and the rock was rough and craggy. They had been flying for half an hour and Jamie was beginning to doubt whether they'd ever get out, when he finally saw sunlight up ahead.

The tunnel emerged on a mountainside. If they hadn't had Sunray it would have been a long and dangerous climb down, but luckily they were able to swoop like a giant eagle into the clearing far below.

'Where are we?' said Jamie.

'I don't know,' admitted Balthazar.

'Cloud Mountains,' said Adeel, bringing Sunray in to land. 'We came here on a field trip last summer.'

'We need to get back to the Academy as quickly as possible to warn everybody,' said Jamie.

Sunray bucked and collapsed onto the ground.

'He's exhausted,' said Adeel, giving Sunray a pat. 'He's not used to carrying three people. He'll need a rest before we make the journey back to the Academy.'

'Five minutes,' said Jamie as they all jumped off the wilting magic carpet, glad to feel solid cloud under their feet for a while. 'Then we need to leave!'

Jamie leant against a cloud tree and shook his head in frustration. He was desperate to get back. Who knew what was happening in the cavern? Dakhil and Dabir had Methuzular – just who they wanted to put their evil plan into action. And they didn't even need Dylan any more. Jamie shuddered and tried not to think about what that might mean.

It took longer for the exhausted magic carpet to recover than any of them expected. The five minutes were more like fifty and even when they were airborne once again and swooping towards the Academy, Sunray was struggling under the weight.

'I knew I shouldn't have had extra chips for lunch,' said Adeel, patting his tummy.

'Can't he go any faster?' said Jamie. 'We need to get back to the Academy before Dakhil.'

Adeel turned and shot Jamie a look. 'Sunray is going as fast as he can,' he snapped. 'Feel free to walk if you like!'

Immediately Jamie felt bad. He didn't mean to take his frustrations out on Sunray – it was Dakhil and Dabir who had made him angry, not the carpet.

'Sorry, Sunray,' said Jamie, giving him a friendly pat. 'I know you're doing your best.'

Eventually, far below them, the Academy loomed into view. Its magnificent turrets sparkled and the building gleamed like gold in the sunlight.

'Everything looks normal,' said Jamie, as Sunray skimmed over the treetops at the edge of the playing fields.

'We need to warn the teachers,' said Adeel. 'Some of them will be powerful enough to help cast the reversal wish.'

Jamie and Balthazar agreed and together they made a list of the teachers who would be brave enough to stand up to Dakhil and Dabir.

When they were close, Adeel landed Sunray in a paddock by the stables, and they ran over to the Academy building.

Jamie was about to push open the heavy cloud doors when they heard voices on the other side.

Balthazar grabbed Jamie and Adeel and pulled them into a cloud bush just as the door opened to reveal Dakhil and Dabir leading Methuzular and Dylan outside.

'We need to help them,' said Adeel, beginning to stand up.

'We're too late,' Jamie said, pulling him back down with a heavy heart. 'Methuzular is already on their side.'

'How do you know?' asked Adeel, struggling against Jamie's grip.

'Look at him,' said Jamie quietly. 'He's not chained up. He could escape if he wanted to. There's only one explanation for it: Dakhil and Dabir know he'll do whatever they tell him. Don't you see? He's already hypnotised.'

Adeel's face fell as he took in the blank look of the headmaster. Jamie had hoped Methuzular would find a way to save the day, but if the most powerful genie in Lampville couldn't resist Dakhil, Dabir and their hypno-wish, what hope did anyone else have? Suddenly Jamie felt lost. He didn't have his wise old friend to turn to for help and the genie world was on the brink of disaster. How could they

possibly put a stop to
Dakhil and Dabir's
plans now?

As Dakhil and Dabir
led Methuzular and
Dylan past the cloud
bush, they could
overhear their
conversation.

'That's every
teacher in the
school under our
control,' said Dabir with a grin.

'Just like I planned,' said Dakhil, rubbing his
hands together. 'I knew calling a staff meeting
would be the best way to do it. No teacher can
resist that, or Methuzular's wish-granting power!'

Dakhil turned to Methuzular. 'Well done, slave!'
he said.

'Thank you, master,' intoned Methuzular. His
voice had that same dreamy, faraway quality that
Jamie recognised from when Balthazar had been
hypnotised.

'Did you hear that?' hissed Balthazar. 'Every teacher under their spell! Who's going to help us now?'

Jamie put a finger to his lips. He wanted to hear what Dabir and Dakhil were plotting next.

'Just the pupils left here,' said Dakhil. 'Then we head to Lampville. Our hypno-wish will spread like a virus, and soon every genie in the world will be under our power.'

Jamie shuddered at the thought.

Dakhil turned to Methuzular. 'Call an emergency assembly,' he instructed. 'You can hypnotise all the children at once to do our bidding!'

'Of course, master,' said Methuzular, giving Dakhil an obedient nod as he went back inside.

'Slave!' barked Dakhil, turning to Dylan. 'Get my flying carpet ready. I want to travel to Lampville in style.'

'Yes, master,' said Dylan, and ran off towards the stables as Dakhil and Dabir strutted after him. When they were gone, Adeel turned to Jamie. 'What are we going to do?' he said. 'We can't overpower the whole school!'

'We need to use the reverse hyno-wish,' Jamie said. 'It's the only way. But Methuzular said it was very difficult and that it would take even him a while to collect his strength. We need a very powerful genie to make the wish. But with all the teachers hypnotised too, who?'

They all thought hard.

'We need my gran,' Jamie said suddenly. 'She'll be able to make the wish.

Jamie's gran was Methuzular's sister. She had once been a powerful genie herself but had given it all away when she fell in love with Jamie's  granddad. She had wished herself human so that she could be with him for ever. She had once wished herself back into being a genie to save Lampville.

Jamie led the way as they crept down the corridors towards Farah's classroom and the Portal of Dreams. The Academy seemed eerily quiet.

'I bet he's got all the trainee genies confined to dorms in case they figure out something's wrong,' said Adeel, noticing the lack of chatter and the absence of genies running around, practising their favourite wishes.

As soon as they got to Farah's classroom, Jamie sensed something was wrong. The door was hanging off its hinges and books were scattered all over the floor. Jamie held up a hand and Balthazar and Adeel stopped behind him.

'What's going on?' asked Balthazar.

'I have a bad feeling about this,' said Adeel.

'It might be a trap,' said Balthazar.

'I'll look – you two stay here,' said Jamie.

Jamie stuck his head around the door and took a peek inside. He half-expected to find a hypnotised teacher waiting for him, but what he saw was much worse. The room was in complete disarray and the portal was standing in the middle of the class – smashed to pieces.

Suddenly Adeel and Balthazar were at Jamie's shoulder.

'What's the matter?' asked Balthazar. 'You look like you've seen a ghost.'

Jamie could only point. How was he going to get to Gran now?

'Why have they done that?' said Adeel, shaking his head in disbelief.

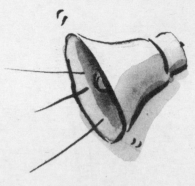

'Dakhil told me he was going to get rid of the connections between the genie world and the human world,' said Jamie quietly. 'He said he wasn't angry with humans any more – his anger was purely for genies now. He said he was going to destroy every portal and forget all about us. I just didn't think he would have started so soon.'

'What are we going to do?' asked Balthazar.

Jamie looked at the floor in despair. There was no way back to his gran now. In fact, he wasn't sure how he and Dylan were ever going to get home. Of course, that might not matter if they were hypnotised – or dead.

Jamie shook the gloomy thoughts from his mind and fixed his friends with a determined stare. 'Gran can't help us now,' he said with a grim nod. 'We're going to have to stop this ourselves.'

'But how?' asked Adeel.

Suddenly the Academy's speakers crackled into life and the voice of Methuzular boomed out.

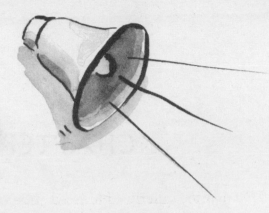

'All students to the playing field for an emergency assembly!' he ordered. 'Now!'

Jamie looked to his friends. He had absolutely no idea how they could stop Dahkil and Dabir, but they had to think of something fast or the genie way of life they all knew and loved would be gone for ever.

CHAPTER 12

Suddenly the corridors were filled with genie pupils all making their way towards the playing fields.

Balthazar held out his hands and blocked the corridor. 'It's a trap!' he said. 'Methuzular's been hypnotised!'

The genies looked shocked for a moment, and then began to laugh.

'Good one, Balthazar! You always tell the best jokes,' said a blond genie.

'You'd better get out of the way, though – we don't want to get a detention for being late!' a short genie with thick brown hair said, ducking between Balthazar's legs.

'It's true!' shouted Adeel to the crowd. 'You have to believe him!'

'Yeah!' laughed a red-headed genie. 'Just like the time he said the Academy was on fire because he saw smoke billowing by the windows and it turned out it was just a bit foggy!'

'Why won't they listen?' said Balthazar, as more genies barged past.

'With your track record, do you blame them?' said Jamie. 'We can't worry about them now; we have to stop Methuzular!'

Jamie, Adeel and Balthazar joined the throng of genies and headed into the Academy grounds. Instead of following them to the playing field where they knew Methuzular was waiting to hypnotise them, they made their way down an overgrown path to plot and plan behind a boulder.

The genies lined up in their year groups in front of their teachers. When everyone was ready,

Methuzular gave a nod and Dakhil and Dabir
stepped out from behind a tree. The genies gasped
in surprise when they saw them, with mutterings
and boos rippling through the crowd. They were
both infamous in the genie world for their evil-
doing. Dakhil had been a cruel and deceitful
headmaster and had made Dabir headboy. Dabir

had used his power to make his fellow pupils answer his every beck and call. No one was sorry to see them banished to a bottle at the bottom of the sea by Methuzular and the Genie Congress, and everyone had presumed that was the last they would see of them for a very long time. To find them both standing in the Academy grounds as if

nothing had happened was a shock for everybody.

Methuzular held out his hands for calm. 'Fear not!' he said in his dreamy, faraway voice. 'Dakhil and Dabir are changed characters. I have called this assembly to welcome them back to the Academy.'

One or two of the young genies were shaking their heads – as far as they were concerned Dakhil and Dabir could never make up for what they had done – but before they had chance to say so, Methuzular started to work the hypno-wish. Dakhil and Dabir had obviously taught him well, and Jamie watched as a huge cloud of sparkles began to build and sweep towards the confused-looking students.

'We have to do something!' said Jamie.

'We could bash Methuzular on the head,' Adeel said. 'It worked to free Balthazar. I could use this – it's certainly heavy enough.' Adeel removed the tiny Book of Wishes from his waistcoat pocket and wished it back to its normal size.

'We'd never get close enough,' said Jamie. 'Dakhil would kill us first! And besides, I don't

think we can rely on a blow to the head to work all the time. I think it was lucky Balthazar wasn't really hurt.'

'We'll just have to try the reversal spell ourselves,' Jamie said. They began to flick through the book, searching for the right wish.

'Hypnotism, hypnotism,' Balthazar mumbled as he turned over the pages. 'H . . . I . . . P . . .'

'That's not how you spell hypnotism,' said Jamie, but Balthazar wasn't listening.

'I've got hip replacement, hip-hop, hippy,' Balthazar looked up. 'We could turn Methuzular into a hip-hopping hippy?' he offered.

'Give me that!' said Jamie, snatching the book away. 'It's "Y", not "I"!' he said.

'Why?' said Balthazar.

'Yes "Y"!' said Jamie.

'Why "Y"?' asked Baltahzar.

'Just because,' snapped Jamie flicking through the pages.

'Hypno-wish – reversing,' said Adeel, reading the book over his shoulder. 'That's the one! Go and do it, Balthazar.'

All the colour drained from Balthazar's face.

'Me?' spluttered Balthazar. 'Why me?'

'Because you're the oldest,' said Adeel. 'You've got most experience!'

'Me! Cast a wish like that?!' said Balthazar. 'No way! Anything might happen! I might turn Methuzular into a mountain goat or something! You do it.'

Adeel shook his head. 'I've got to guard the Book of Wishes,' he said. 'If anything goes wrong, I have to be alive to take it to a hiding place.'

'Then I'll try to do it,' said Jamie, taking the book and studying the page. He breathed a transformation wish at his finger, turning it briefly into a pen, and scrawled the wish on his other hand.

'Good idea, Jamie,' said Adeel. 'You're Methuzular's great nephew after all!'

'He's more than great,' exclaimed Balthazar. 'He's blooming brilliant!'

'No, I meant Methuzular's his . . .' explained Adeel. 'Oh, never mind!'

Jamie studied the wish on his hand.

Wish of power,
wish of might
Help me make my
good friend right
Rid him of the wish
in his brain...

'It's worth trying, Jamie,' encouraged Adeel. 'You've got more magic in your little finger than the rest of us put together. You've just got to be confident!'

Adeel was right. Some of Methuzular's magnificent magic was clearly in Jamie's genes. Jamie hadn't had much practise, but the wishes he had made had got him out of trouble before. He just had to trust his instincts. But even if he had the power, he had very little experience. It was unlikely he'd manage – but he had to try.

'I'll need help,' said Jamie. 'As Methuzular is always saying, the element of surprise is key!'

'What do you need us to do?' asked Adeel.

'If I'm going to grant the wish, then I need you

to cause a diversion,' said Jamie. 'While everyone's looking at you, I'll try to get close enough to Methuzular to reverse the hypno-wish.'

'I have an idea for a distraction,' Adeel said.

'How will I know when you're ready?' asked Jamie.

'Oh, you'll know,' Adeel answered with a mischievous grin, and dragged Balthazar off down the path.

Jamie stayed crouched behind the boulder and waited. Methuzular was walking through the crowd of students, checking that the wish had caught each and every one of them. Jamie couldn't bear to look at their blank stares, and felt angry watching Dakhil and Dabir smile wickedly in delight.

Suddenly a cry rang out across the playing fields. 'Up here, bozos!'

Jamie recognised Balthazar's voice. He looked up to see where it had come from and gasped in amazement when he saw Balthazar zooming across the sky on Sunray with Adeel at his side.

All eyes were suddenly on the two genies. Balthazar wished up an enormous bowl of ice cream and, using the scoop as a catapult, started to pelt the young genies. The hypnotised pupils barely reacted but Dakhil and Dabir were glaring upwards.

Adeel steered Sunray towards Dakhil, and Balthazar let rip with a large glob of strawberry and vanilla. It splatted onto Dakhil's head and he and Dabir ran for cover.

'Do you want a flake with that?' taunted Balthazar, firing off another scoop.

'Stop them!' bellowed Dakhil, dripping with ice cream and pointing into the sky.

'Stop them!' echoed Methuzular obediently.

The hypnotised trainee genies gave chase, scattering willy nilly as they tried desperately to keep up with the swooping Sunray.

Jamie seized his chance. With the young genies scattered like headless chickens, there was a clear route to Methuzular. He sprang from his hiding place, and sprinted towards the hypnotised headmaster.

As he weaved around pupils and dodged ice-cream bombs, Jamie began to read out the wish, trying hard to take his mind to that special place where magic could happen. In all the noise and confusion it was harder than ever!

'*Wish of power, wish of might!*' Jamie tried to shout over the chaos, but each word he spoke was a struggle and he found it impossible to concentrate. It was as if he was being pushed away from the magical place in his mind.

Out of the corner of his eye he saw Dakhil blow a mighty wish cloud towards Sunray and his two friends.

'Whoa!' screamed Balthazar as a fire-breathing dragon emerged from the cloud.

Adeel did his best to get away, but the dragon was too fast. It let out a plume of flame, singeing

Sunray's tassels. The carpet bucked in pain and Adeel and Balthazar were tossed from the carpet's back, landing in a tree.

Jamie desperately wanted to help them, but he couldn't get distracted. He had to finish the wish. He blocked everything from his mind but the spell.

'*Help me make my good friend right!*' he continued, gasping. He was halfway through.

Methuzular had noticed him and turned to face him, but so had Dabir. Jamie ran faster.

'*Rid him of the wish in his brain!*' Jamie struggled to speak, the words barely audible.

Dabir elbowed Dakhil and pointed.

'No!' shouted Dakhil, realising what Jamie was up to. 'Stop!'

Jamie was almost there. With Methuzular back to normal and on his side they could put everything right. He opened his mouth to say the last line.

'I said stop!' yelled Dakhil.

'Or your friends die!

All of them!'

Jamie turned to look and the last line of the wish stuck in his throat. Dakhil was holding Dylan by the neck.

'One word from me,' said Dakhil, 'and he and your carpet-riding clowns are gone!'

Jamie didn't know what to do. He had to save Dylan, but he couldn't leave all the genies to their terrible fate. He had to take the risk, and free Methuzular.

He turned back to the headmaster, and opened his mouth to speak the final line.

But he'd waited too long. At that moment, a hand clamped over his mouth, silencing Jamie, and squashing his only chance to save them all.

Jamie could feel the wish fade away. Dakhil's hypno-wish wish was just too powerful.

His plan had failed.

CHAPTER 13

As the rough hands grabbed Jamie, he saw some other genies had pulled Balthazar and Adeel from the tree. They looked at him in despair as they were marched to Dakhil and Dabir and flung to the ground. The hypnotised genies formed a circle around them and Methuzular pushed his way through to stand next to his evil masters.

'I have no quarrel with the human world,' said

Dakhil. 'It's only the genies who need to worry.'

'But I am part genie!' said Jamie defiantly. 'My gran was a genie, remember?'

Dabir gave him a kick with the tip of his foot. 'You're no genie,' he spat. 'You never have been and you never will be.'

'If you'd kept out of it I'd have let you live and sent you home,' said Dakhil. 'But now . . .'

'You were never going to let us go home!' snapped Jamie. 'You've destroyed the school Portal of Dreams, and I'm sure you'll destroy the others as soon as you can!'

Dakhil ignored him, and spread his arms wide. 'Methuzular has hypnotised every genie in the Academy. They will do whatever he says – and Methuzular will do whatever I say! We'll teach them the hypno-wish for themselves and Lampville will be under our power by teatime.'

'Teatime? Oh good,' said Dabir. 'They can polish the cherries on our cupcakes.'

Balthazar stood to protest but Dakhil kicked him back to the ground.

'I preferred you hypnotised,' said Dakhil with a

cruel smirk. 'So much easier to handle. We'll soon fix that!'

Dakhil inhaled deeply and blew a hypno-wish over Balthazar. Balthazar's eyes went dull and his jaw slackened as the wish wormed its way in through his ears. Jamie punched the ground in frustration. He hated to see his friend robbed of

his personality. He loved Balthazar's bad jokes and wonky wishes and dreaded to think what Balthazar might get up to under Dakhil's wish.

Dakhil turned to Jamie and Dylan. 'We don't need to hypnotise you. It's time to get rid of you two humans once and for all!' he said.

Dabir scurried to his side. 'Can I help, Dad?' he asked.

Dakhil nodded. 'On three. One . . . two . . .'

Jamie couldn't begin to imagine what horror Dakhil and Dabir would wish on him. He saw a large cloud of sparkles building around Dakhil and Dabir, closed his eyes, and waited.

And waited.

Jamie opened one eye, wondering why Dakhil had not said three, and then he opened the other. He blinked in confusion at what he saw. Dakhil and Dabir were floating helplessly in a swirling cloud of shooting stars, unable to move, but with a look of surprise stuck on their faces. Jamie followed the trail of the cloud and saw it had come from Methuzular!

'Stop!' shouted Dakhil as Methuzular stepped

forward. 'As your master I command you!'

'I am not your servant!' shouted Methuzular. 'I never have been and I never will be!'

Methuzular took two soft balls of wax from his pocket and held them up for Dakhil to see. 'You trapped me in a cage with nothing but a candlestick,' he said, 'but while you were busy

plotting all the
terrible things you
were going to make
me do once I was
your slave, I was
plotting too. I sealed
my ears completely
with wax from the
candle. Your wish
didn't affect me.

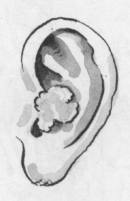

I pretended to be hypnotised until I could be sure
of victory.'

Dakhil's mouth was opening and closing like a
goldfish, but Dabir came to his senses.

'Capture Methuzular,' Dabir shouted at the top
of his voice to all the hypnotised genies.

The genies all looked at him, but not one of
them moved.

Dakhil and Dabir shared a look of panic.

'You needed me to cast a wish so powerful it
would hypnotise the whole school at once,'
Methuzular said to Dakhil to Dabir, 'but because I
cast the wish, not you, they will only obey my

voice, not yours. I have an army of trainee genies on my side! Release Jamie Najar!'

The genie that had been holding Jamie tight obediently let him go.

Jamie got to his feet, shaking.

'I could order all these genies to do what I want,' said Methuzular, 'but I think they can decide for themselves.'

Dabir instantly made a run for the Academy, but Adeel jumped into the air and rugby-tackled him to the ground. With Dabir and Dakhil at his feet, Methuzular took a deep breath and read the wish scrawled on Jamie's hand, loud enough for all to hear.

> *'Wish of power, wish of might,*
> *Help me make my good friends right.*
> *Rid them of the wish in their brain,*
> *Make them who they were again!'*

Methuzular blew the biggest wish cloud Jamie had ever seen. It floated over the heads of the hypnotised genies before plummeting to the ground and shrouding them with sparkles. So powerful was Methuzular's wish, the effect was instantaneous. All the genies started to groan and shake their heads, as if waking from a dream.

Even Dylan blinked in confusion and stood up. 'Where am I?' he said. 'Am I late for lamp polishing class?'

Jamie laughed. He couldn't believe that his best friend knew nothing of the trouble he had caused.

Confusion reigned over the playing fields as the genies tried to figure out what had happened to them. Adeel was holding Dabir tight, but Dakhil managed to shake himself free and bolted.

'Don't let him get away!' shouted Methuzular, blowing a wish in Dakhil's direction, but the evil genie was running so fast he was well out of range before the wish could strike.

Jamie leapt after him, with a pack of genies led by Balthazar and Methuzular just behind.

Dakhil darted round a cloud tree and sprinted across the field. It was then that Jamie realised where he was going. Dakhil was heading for the spooky tumble-down ruin of Alim Tower.

CHAPTER 14

Jamie watched Dakhil disappear through the doorway of Alim tower and followed him inside. The doorway opened onto a spiral staircase and Jamie could hear Dakhil's footsteps clatter above him as he followed him up the stairs.

Dakhil had converted the middle floor of the tower into his own private quarters when he had been headmaster and Jamie was sure that's where he was heading. As he rounded the corner, Jamie saw the door to the office close. Below him, Jamie could hear shouting voices. The other genies had nearly caught up. He was certain Dakhil was trapped.

Jamie pushed open the door and stepped into the tower room. The old desk Dakhil had used stood on a yellow rug, but everything else looked dusty and long-abandoned.

There was no sign of Dakhil.

Jamie took a tentative step into the room to look more carefully, and suddenly the door banged shut behind him.

Jamie turned to find that Dakhil had been hiding behind it all along. Dakhil ran for Jamie and gripped his waistcoat, his face a twisted mask of rage.

'You!' he growled. 'You ruin everything!'

Jamie tried to prise Dakhil's fingers loose but he wasn't letting go.

The tower room door flew open and Methuzular and Balthazar stood framed in the doorway. Other genies gathered behind them, trying to see what was happening.

'Let him go, Dakhil!' boomed Methuzular. 'The game is up!'

Dakhil snarled and shook his head. 'Never!' he spat, clinging on to Jamie. 'You let me go, or Jamie will pay the price! I will blow a wish at him more dangerous than any wish you have ever known. He'll never go home again!'

Jamie found himself shaking in Dakhil's grip. He  had no idea whether Dakhil was bluffing or not, but he wasn't keen to find out. Worse, while Dakhil was holding on to Jamie so tightly, any wish Methuzular might use against Dakhil might affect him too.

'Just let my son and me disappear,' said Dakhil.
Methuzular shook his head. 'I can't do that,
Dakhil. You need to be punished for your crimes.'

'Very well!' snapped Dakhil. 'Then Jamie dies!'

Dakhil glared at Jamie. There was desperation in
his eyes. He knew he and his son were going to be
banished to Lampville Jail for ever and nothing he
did now would make his punishment any worse.
Dakhil breathed in deeply, as if sucking all of the
air out of the room, and prepared to wish.

Jamie's heart began to thump. This was it. He
was never going to see his mum, dad, Baby Paulie
or Gran again. Tears welled in his eyes. He wished
he could just be back at home, in his bedroom or
playing in the garden. Even practising judo with
his next-door neighbours would feel safer than
this!

Suddenly a thought popped into his head. Judo!
In an instant, Jamie shifted his weight, and pushed
Dakhil away from him.

Dakhil staggered but held firm to Jamie. He was
holding Jamie's waistcoat in the same way Josh had
held him before he flipped him. Jamie tried to

remember what the boys had taught him, and suddenly kicked his leg and swiped it across the floor, right underneath Dakhil.

Dakhil had never seen such a thing, and roared as Jamie flung him through the air. He landed on

his back with a thud and Jamie landed on top. Balthazar helped Jamie up off the dazed genie and gave him a big hug while Methuzular and the others restrained Dakhil.

'You have to teach me that!' said Balthazar.

Jamie grinned. Sometimes human skills were more useful than wishes.

Four genies carried Dakhil back down the spiral steps to where Dabir was sitting, still being held by Adeel and surrounded by genies. Dylan was standing by his side.

'Where did you get to?' asked Dylan. 'It's not easy capturing bad genies, you know!'

'Tell me about it,' said Jamie with a smile.

A messenger was sent to Lampville Jail and six guards arrived on fierce-looking magic carpets to take Dakhil and Dabir away. No one was sorry to see them go.

As the genies walked back towards the Academy, Methuzular ruffled Jamie's hair. 'Jamie Najar saves the day again,' he said, laughing. 'You're quite the hero!'

When they got to the Academy, Methuzular took Adeel, Balthazar, Jamie and Dylan to his office.

'We had better be getting home,' said Jamie. 'I think I've had enough excitement for one visit!'

Dylan's face fell. 'But I've only just got here!' he spluttered.

'It's not my fault you don't remember the adventure!' explained Jamie patiently.

'Not fair!' said Dylan, folding his arms in an angry strop. 'It was supposed to be the best wish ever and I missed all the excitement!'

Methuzular rose to his feet and smoothed down his robes. 'You would both be most welcome to stay,' he said. 'In any case, it will take a while to locate another portal to get you home.'

'And it's still night-time back on Earth,' said Balthazar. 'You don't have to be back for ages yet!'

Dylan turned to Jamie. 'Please, Jamie!' he pleaded. 'Your gran's covering for us after all!'

Jamie looked from Dylan to Balthazar to Adeel and finally to Methuzular. How could he disappoint all of his best friends, and his great uncle, in one go? Besides, he had to admit that another few weeks at the Academy sounded like fun. Provided he could have a good night's sleep first, of course!

CHAPTER 15

Jamie and Dylan said goodnight to Balthazar and Methuzular, and Adeel led them up to the dormitories at the top of the Academy. Dylan's eyes boggled as he took in all of the weird and wonderful sights. He had been hypnotised before he had the chance to appreciate all that the Academy had to offer. Dylan was amazed by the beautiful cloud statues that lurked around every corner, the delicious food that was wished up for supper and the wonderfully soft cloud beds that felt like you were lying on thin air.

In Adeel's dormitory, the other genies were all pleased to see them and were full of questions about what had happened and who had done what to whom. Jamie wished everyone up a bowl of his legendary ice cream and they all gathered around his bunk to listen. They shrieked in disgust when he told them all about his rattlesnake tongue and gasped in shock at the tale of Dylan and the spikes of doom.

'Wow!' said Dylan when Jamie had finished his story. 'I had no idea any of that was happening! You must be exhausted!'

'I am quite,' said Jamie, stifling a yawn.

Jamie finished his ice cream and clambered into the cloud bed. It felt softer and more comfortable than ever.

Jamie and Dylan slept soundly all night, and the following morning Adeel took them down for breakfast. You could eat whatever you wished for in the Academy and Dylan asked Adeel to scoop up some cloud and turn it into a bacon sandwich. After breakfast, they went to Methuzular's classroom for wish-granting lessons.

Over the next few weeks, Jamie and Dylan had a wonderful time. Jamie was able to brush up on all of the skills he had learnt on his first visit and Dylan was able to take his first steps towards becoming a genie. In between all of the mint tea brewing, lamp polishing, magic carpet racing, and wish matches, Jamie, Dylan, Adeel and Balthazar became the firmest of friends.

Every evening after school Jamie, Dylan and Adeel would take it in turns to race around the magic carpet track on Threadbare and Sunray while Balthazar timed them with a stopwatch. Dylan proved to be just as good at carpet racing as

Jamie and their nailbiting races soon became something that every genie in the Academy gathered to watch.

Jamie was really pleased to be able to share his genie life with his best human friend, but all too soon, lessons at the Academy drew to a close, and it was time for the end of term banquet in the Great Hall. All of the genies and their teachers got changed into their finest waistcoats and assembled in the hall for a feast.

Methuzular sat at a top table with the other teachers and Jamie and Dylan sat with their

friends on long benches. The tables were lit with
candles and delicious food was piled high in front
of them. Dylan licked his lips as he eyed the cakes,

sweets and jellies and tried to decide what to taste
first. In the end, he scooped one of each onto a big
plate and tucked in.

Above them, the statues of famous genies
seemed to look down on them proudly, and as
everyone ate, acrobats tumbled, jugglers juggled
and musicians played strange and wonderful music.

Once the feast was over, Methuzular stood and

called the room to order. 'Before we go our separate ways,' he boomed, 'I have an announcement.'

The room fell silent.

'As you know, we have been joined by Jamie and Dylan for this term,' he continued. 'Jamie has done so much for genies and we owe him our of thanks. He has saved me from dungeons, saved the Academy from ruin and saved us all from becoming slaves to a very mean master. Not to mention giving us the most delicious ice cream we have ever tasted!' he added.

A laugh echoed round the hall.

'We thought it was about time we acknowledged our debt to him,' said Methuzular. He nodded towards the side of the room, where an object was covered in a white sheet.

'Dakhil, for all his bad points, did have one good idea,' explained Methuzular, walking towards it and tugging at the sheet. 'A statue of Jamie Najar in the Great Hall seems like a very wise thing to do!'

Jamie gasped as he gazed at the statue. It looked just like him! He was wearing his genie waistcoat and was holding a battered old teapot under his arm

— the teapot in which Balthazar had been trapped, and which had introduced him to the genie world.

Dylan gave him a nudge. 'It's the spitting image,' he said playfully. 'Right down to the sticky out ears and the goofy teeth!'

Methuzular raised his glass in a toast and the other genies did the same. 'To Jamie Najar,' he boomed. 'The first human to ever attend the

Academy and who saved us all!'

The room erupted into cheers and Jamie blinked back tears of joy as he bowed and acknowledged the applause.

When the banquet was over, Methuzular called Jamie and Dylan over to him. 'A new portal has been delivered to my office,' he said quietly. 'Dawn is breaking over planet Earth and you will soon be missed.'

Methuzular led the two boys to his office and the replacement Portal of Dreams.

Balthazar and Adeel were waiting there, ready to say goodbye.

'Would you care to do the honours, Jamie?' asked Methuzular.

Jamie nodded and

guided the portal towards his house. The portal worked like a clever video game – the right hand moved the picture left and right and the left hand moved it forward and back. Jamie manipulated the image on the screen like a true genie and soon they were zooming down Jamie's street, past the corner shop and the flickering street light and into Jamie's bedroom. His bed hadn't been slept in and the campbed that had been put there for Dylan remained untouched. Light was beginning to stream through the gap in the curtains.

'Goodbye, Balthazar,' said Jamie, giving his friend a hug.

'Thanks for everything, Jamie,' said Balthazar. 'If it weren't for you I'd still be a zombie.'

'Which might be safer for us all,' added Methuzular with a chuckle.

'Come back soon,' said Adeel as he gave Jamie a hug.

'Me too?' asked Dylan.

Methuzular ruffled Dylan's hair. 'You're always welcome too.' He smiled. 'Just try not to cause so much trouble with your wishes next time!'

Then Jamie took Dylan's hand and together they walked through the portal and into Jamie's bedroom. Jamie felt his tummy tingle as the portal rippled.

They looked back to see Balthazar, Adeel and Methuzular gathered around waving, before the portal disappeared in a puff of smoke.

Jamie and Dylan had only just climbed into their beds when Jamie's mum bustled into the room with two mugs of tea. 'Wakey, wakey, sleepyheads!' she said, popping the mugs on Jamie's desk. 'There's a day full of adventure waiting out there if you go and look for it!'

Dylan and Jamie shared a knowing smile. They'd had more adventure than she would ever know!

CHAPTER 16

After breakfast it was time for Dylan to go home. Jamie walked with him to the front gate.

'That was amazing,' said Dylan. 'Do you ever think we'll go back?'

Jamie paused at the gate and thought for a moment. 'I don't know,' he said. 'Perhaps if there's trouble we might be called on again. Perhaps it would be nice to visit when there wasn't too!'

Dylan's face broke into a broad smile. 'Let's hope so!' he said. 'And next time I'll help. I do a mean Chinese burn, you know!'

Jamie was just about to head back inside when Oliver, Will and Josh came out of their front door. They were taking Baxter for a walk and the dog was pulling eagerly on his lead.

'There you are!' said Will. 'Where did you get to yesterday?'

'My judo moves scared him off!' said Josh.

Jamie smiled sheepishly. 'I had to go. Sorry I didn't say goodbye.'

'We thought you'd disappeared into a hedge,' said Will.

'Or vanished into thin air!' said Josh.

Jamie joined in with their laughter, a little nervously.

'Who vanishes into thin air?' snorted Oliver. 'Honestly, Josh, you and your imagination!'

Baxter yelped and pulled Oliver towards the gate.

'Gotta go, Jamie! Someone needs a stick throwing!' said Will as they headed for the gate.

'Come over later and I'll show you my latest

move,' called Josh. 'Unless you're a chicken!'

They disappeared in a flurry of barking, wagging and tugging.

Jamie was glad it was Sunday. He was exhausted after his term in the Academy. He was planning a nice relaxing day in his bedroom with a good book and a DVD. As he made his way back upstairs, his gran was coming down.

'How was the Academy?' she whispered. 'As exciting as ever?'

'It was the most exciting yet,' said Jamie. 'Dahkil and Dabir Ganim returned!'

Gran's eyebrows nearly flew off her forehead in surprise.

'But don't worry — they're in Lampville Jail now.'

'Really!' she said. 'And what about the statue?'

Jamie nodded and Gran punched the air in delight.

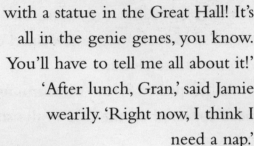

'Who'd have thought?' she said. 'My grandson with a statue in the Great Hall! It's all in the genie genes, you know. You'll have to tell me all about it!'

'After lunch, Gran,' said Jamie wearily. 'Right now, I think I need a nap.'

Gran tapped her nose conspiratorially. 'Mum's the word,' she said with a wink. 'Or should that be Gran's the word, eh?'

Jamie giggled and headed up to his bedroom. He was about to flop onto his bed and stick on his favourite Top Gear DVD when he noticed something strange on his bedroom table. A small object had been placed there covered in a cloth. He lifted the cloth and found a miniature version of the Great Hall statue staring back at him. It was identical in every way, and seemed to be made out of pure white cloud.

As he picked it up to examine it, Balthazar's head appeared on the face of the statue.

'Thought you might like a little memento. Until the next time, Jamie Najar!'

Balthazar disappeared and Jamie placed the cloud statue back on his bedside table and sank onto his bed. As he closed his eyes, his head was filled with dreams of powerful genies, wonderful wishes and daring magic carpet races. Who knew what adventure was just around the corner?

Have you read . . .

GENIE IN TRAINING

When Jamie's gran gives him a battered old
teapot he reckons she's gone doolally!
But then he cleans it, and out pops
Balthazar Najar, a banished genie!

Balthazar grants three wishes, but for the last one,
Jamie accidentally wishes he was a genie . . .
He's whisked off to genie school where
an angry headmaster, a suspiciously friendly
snake and deadly magic carpet races
are the least of his worries!

GENIE IN TROUBLE

There's big trouble in the genie town of
Lampville-upon-Cloud, and Balthazar needs
his human friend Jamie to come back and help!

The bad genies have taken over, thrown the old
headmaster of the Genie Academy in jail
and are planning to take over the human world.
But what can Jamie do about it?
And with mean wishes being granted all over
the place, how will they avoid being turned
into figburgers – or worse?!

It's going to take more than magic
to put things right . . .

WISHING FOR MORE?

Come and explore
for fun and games,
book news and much, much more!

PICCADILLYPRESS.CO.UK/ GENIEACADEMY